ANOTHER BLUE HOLE

by Allen Wayne Ross

***

This book is a work of fiction. Characters, names, places, incidents, and actions are from the author's imagination. Any resemblance to actual persons, places or events is strictly coincidental.

***

DEDICATION

This book is Dedicated to my nephew Brian who is serving in our military in Afghanistan. President Ronald Reagan made the following quote about the Marines, but it applies equally to all branches of the military, and it especially applies to my nephew Brian: " Some people wonder all their lives if they've made a difference. The Marines don't have that problem."

Thank you for your unselfish service which allows all of us to sleep better at night.

You are making a difference!

Freedom is never more than one generation away from extinction.....Ronald Reagan

Chapter 1

Richard St.Clair ambled into the Ganister Police department. Assistant Chief Galen Farr who was sitting at the Chief's desk reading the newspaper, with his feet comfortably on the desk, jumped to his feet when the intruder entered, dropping the newspaper onto the open box of doughnuts and nearly spilling the steaming cup of coffee.

After a brief hesitation, Assistant Chief Farr spoke, "Mayor, you alright?"

"Yeah, why?" came the response.

Galen Farr hesitated again. The reason for his confusion was the man standing in front of him. Richard St.Clair was wearing several days worth of facial hair, sloppy blue jeans, a wrinkled shirt, and hadn't appeared to have combed his hair in days. His normal appearance would have been quite the opposite. Normally he was clean shaven, sporting a button down shirt with colorful necktie and khaki pants. And his hair would have been combed.

"You look different, Mayor," was all the Assistant Chief could say.

"Yeah, whatever," Richard began, "you look like you're making yourself at home at the Chief's desk."

The crimson color spread across Galen's face as he appeared to be looking for an answer, however, Richard didn't give him time to speak as he continued, "look, raise your right hand and repeat after me."

The Assistant Chief did as he was told and raised his hand.

"I solemnly swear to uphold the laws of the United States of America, the Commonwealth of Pennsylvania, and the Borough of Ganister. I will do nothing to tarnish the position of Chief of Police of Ganister. So help me God." After the Assistant Chief said the words, Richard St.Clair tossed him a gold badge, "Congratulations, your the new Chief of Police."

Galen Farr stood quietly admiring the gold badge, then rubbing it vigorously against his shirt to bring out the shine, "Thank you, Mayor."

"Listen, Galen, I'm leaving town for a few days. Don't do anything to embarass me. Don't do anything to cause me any grief or make my phone ring. Okay?"

"You can count on me, Mayor," the new Chief stammered as he took off his old silver badge and pinned on the new gold one.

"Where are you going Mayor?" Galen inquired.

Richard looked down towards the floor and responded in a hushed voice, "Pamela's will stated her ashes were to be put in the Caribbean Sea. I must honor her wishes."

Richard's wife Pamela had recently passed away following a brief struggle with cancer which she unfortunately lost. Ever since then Richard had been lost. He had considered suicide but couldn't follow through. And to date he hasn't been himself, floundering around like a fish out of water.

As Richard turned to leave, the new Chief said to him, "Mayor, since I'm the new Chief, I feel my first act must be to close the Billy Bollinger case."

Billy Bollinger was the son of the previous Chief of Police. Billy was being watched closely by state and federal authorities as an integral player in the distribution of drugs in the small town of Ganister. Billy worked on the ambulance crew and would pick up drugs in the ambulance out of town then bring them back to town and sell them. The Chief knew his son was soon to be arrested so he arranged for him to leave town and go to Florida to live with a relative. Richard saw Billy leaving town, followed him, and gave his a car a little tap driving Billy off the road. Billy was eventually found with two bullet holes in his forehead. When Mayor St.Clair was questioned by Chief Bollinger and the state detective, he admitted pushing Billy's car off the road. He also admitted placing a gun to Billy's forehead but not pulling the trigger. Plus he admitted to giving Billy a bloody nose. All this was done because Billy had attempted to manhandle Richard's wife Pamela on a beach in Aruba after dark and stealing her favorite necklace in the process, making a mistake or two and having Richard find out about it. The Chief learning of the events and especially regarding his dead son, knew exactly who he wanted to see put in jail, that being his own boss, Mayor Richard St.Clair. The Chief broke into Richard's home early one morning on the pretense of arresting him and ended up getting himself shot by Detective Brown of the Pennsylvania State Police and federal undercover agent, and best friend to Richard, Bobby Morrow.

So the case of who killed Billy Bollinger has been languishing ever since.

"You probably should," replied Richard.

"Then Mayor, I will need to ask you some questions," Chief Farr responded.

"I have already been questioned. You can read the report."

"But, I really feel I should personally interview you, Mayor."

"And you can. When I get back from the Caribbean," the Mayor stated as he again turned to leave.

"But,.."

But it was too late as Richard closed the door behind him leaving a dumbstruck new Chief of Police staring after the closed door.

Galen gathered his thoughts after a moment and sat back down at the desk. This time not putting his feet up on the desk as it now was his desk. He opened the drawer, pulled out the manila folder marked, Billy Bollinger, and began to read through each page. First was the interview with Richard St.Clair. All the routine questions were asked and the answers appeared very believable. Just as Galen turned to the next page, he was hit by a thought, "there was never any ballistics test done on the Mayor's gun." He quickly flipped trough the papers to the Coroners report. Two holes to the forehead at very close range as evidenced by the powder burns. Two slugs were removed from the headrest of the vehicle. Both slugs were 38 caliber. Chief Farr had been with Mayor St.Clair on several occasions when the Mayor had his gun with him. He carried a snubnose 38 revolver. And yet, no ballistics test on the gun to rule him in or out. "There's a loose end," Chief Farr said to himself. Going back to the papers right after the interview with Mayor St.Clair, he found an interview with Bobby Morrow. Bobby was the Mayor's best friend, the local part-time dentist, and as everyone now knew, a federal undercover agent. Apparently Bobby Morrow had come along after Billy's car had crashed and he stated that the victim had already been shot. Chief Farr now wondered about two things. One, it's quite a coincidence that the Mayor's best friend comes along, and , two, what kind of gun does he carry? No answers in the report. "Another loose end," Chief Farr says to himself again.Then there is the Coroner's report. No other persons interviewed? The ambulance responded, who called that in? No copy of the 911 report. "Another loose end," Farr said to himself, "this thing has more holes in it than swiss cheese."

Chief Farr began plotting his agenda. He would interview Bobby Morrow. He would get the 911 tapes. He would go to the scene of the crime and see if there could have been any other witnesses. And, yes, as soon as the Mayor gets back, he will re-interview him. "Probably should have never left him leave town," he said to himself, "damn!"

He who knows best knows how little he knows.....Thomas Jefferson.

Chapter 2

Bobby Morrow was a very early riser. Not necessarily because he wanted to, but because he had problems sleeping ever since his tour in Vietnam. That was where he and Richard St.Clair became such close friends. They were advance operations personnel trudging through the jungles of Vietnam risking death every minute they were there. Bobby managed to amass quite a few medals for his acts of bravery, but now he paid the price. The sleepless nights. So he was up early letting Duke, his huge hunk of a dog out for his morning ritual when his phone rang. One look at the number glowing on the screen of the cell phone and Bobby understood who would be calling at this early an hour. "Colonel," he said.

"Bobby, I have a new assignment for you."

"What's up, Colonel?"

"We have a man in Bonaire, in the Netherland Antilles, Clint Armstrong."

"Yes, I know him. He served with Richard and I, and Richard and Pamela used to go each year to Bonaire snorkeling. Then one year my wife and I went with them and we ran into Wildman Armstrong."

"Yes, well, he's dead," the Colonel said with bit of a hiss in his voice.

"I'm sorry to hear that, Colonel."

"So's his wife. I want the bastard that did this. I want you to deliver him to me, dead or alive."

"What sort of operation was Wildman Armstrong running?"

"If you've been to Bonaire then you know that it is a haven for divers and snorkelers. Clint Armstrong's cover was he ran a dive operation but unlike the other ones on the island. The resorts there take divers to many spots around the island but all on the leeward side of the island. Wildman Armstrong took divers to the wild side of the island, where the sharks play. Where it's dangerous. He enjoyed it and even made money at it but most importantly it put him right where we needed him. The drug cartels in South America run drugs by boat up to Curacao and Bonaire then get them onto planes to go into the US. Armstrong was making some real inroads into finding us the source of those drugrunners. Now, suddenly he shows up dead. I don't believe in coincidences. Take care of this Bobby!"

11

The phone went dead. Bobby stared at the cell in his hand for a moment then pressed the end button. "Guess I better pack my swim suit," he said to himself.

He was about to call out the door to his dog Duke when the phone rang again.

"Yeah," he said into the phone.

"Mr. Morrow, this is Chief Galen Farr of the Ganister Police Department."

"Chief?, Galen when did you get promoted?" Bobby asked.

"Just a minute ago. The Mayor came in and swore me in then left me with the Billy Bollinger case to complete," Chief Farr responded.

"Well, Congratulations, Chief," Bobby told him, "what can I do for you?"

"I need to re-interview you as part of the Bollinger case."

"Sure, no problem. I'll call you as soon as I get back into town."

Chief Farr was feeling anxious about the lack of respect he seemed to be getting so far, "I need to talk with you today, Bobby."

"Sorry, government business. I'm heading for the airport."

"But....." Bobby Morrow had already hung up the phone. For the second time this morning Chief Farr was left talking to himself.

Bobby Morrow turned his mind to Wildman Clint Armstrong. They first met right after Bobby and Richard had traversed around the Parrots Beak from Cambodia into Vietnam, where Richard nearly got shot, except Bobby had been keeping an eye on him and was able to shoot the North Vietnamese who had Richard in his sights before the North Vietnamese could pull the trigger. After that they ran into Wildman Armstrong. He was a most impressive person, built like a wedge. A big wedge. He stood probably six foot three with broad square shoulders, a small waist and arms the size of most men's legs. His short buzz cut blond hair and the girly tattoo on his bicep that he liked to make dance as he flexed his muscles. Wildman knew no fear and never lost a fight to anyone, until Bobby came along. Wildman wanted to be sure Bobby and Richard knew their place when they met up with him so he let it be known that he was the man. Bobby, having been fed up with soaking wet clothes, jungle rot growing on his feet, and the lack of a good meal was in no mood to listen to Wildman, so he walked right up to him, stomped on his foot, and when Wildman leaned over to grab his foot, Bobby smacked him on both sides of his head at the same time, with open palms, nearly bursting his ear drums. The bewildered Wildman was left staring blankly at Bobby who grabbed Wildman by the back of the head and rammed that head into his rising knee. Wildman dropped like a sack of potatoes. Bobby sauntered off to find some dry clothes, and Richard just stood there smiling. No one else felt any desire to challenge the Wildman so he continued to rule the roost, but he did respect Bobby from that point on. They became very good friends, and after the war, when the Colonel called Bobby to do some undercover work for the federal government, Bobby recommended Wildman Armstrong also be approached. Richard was approached but he turned the Colonel down as he no longer felt the need for the excitement like Bobby and Wildman.

One way to make sure crime doesn't pay would be to let the government run it............Ronald Reagan

Chapter 3

Chief Galen Farr grabbed the keys to the squad car and left the office for the 911 station after making the call to the judge's office to arrange for the warrant he would need to get the 911 tapes. After arriving, he had to ring the buzzer and produce his badge to gain entry. The security at the 911 center was at a very high level. Chief Galen Farr then sat with an operator and listened to the tapes from the day that Billy Bollinger was shot.

The first call in was from a man who refused to give his name stating that there was an automobile accident along Route 866 and the ambulance needed to get there quickly. After a few minutes there was a second call in. This time the caller identified himself, "there is a dead man in a car on Route 866 approximately 2 miles west of the Ganister borough line. Sir, can I have your name came the 911 operator's response. Bobby Morrow. Please send the ambulance right away," and the line went dead. Galen now had confirmation that Morrow was at the scene, making him even more of a suspect than before. And who was the first caller. Galen thought he might know the voice but so far no name was popping into his head.

"Thank you," Chief Farr said and left the 911 center.

On his drive back to Ganister he stopped by the exact spot where Billy Bollinger's car had been off the road. He slowly turned his body looking outward to see if any homes were within viewing distance that might produce a witness. Just one. Up on the small hill was the home of Mrs. Geuring. She was a widow that had lived there for quite a while and everyone in Ganister knew her.

Galen drove up to her house and knocked on the door.

"Mornin' Mrs. Geuring," Chief Farr said when she answered the door.

"Well Good Morning, Galen," she replied as she smoothed back her gray hair with her right hand, "what brings you out this way?"

"I wanted to see if ...."

Mrs. Geuring interrupted, "Oh pardon me, where are my manners?Please come in, Galen. Would you like a cup of coffee?"

"Well, thank you ma'm, don't mind if I do," Galen said as he entered the house and closed the squeaky screen door and wooden outer door behind himself.

Mrs. Geuring led him straight to the kitchen table and poured him a cup of coffee. Then she topped off her cup and sat down, "please sit!"

Galen sat and unable to resist the aroma coming from the steaming cup, took a long drink.

"Mrs. Geuring....."

Again she interrupted him, "Galen, just call me Grammy like everyone else."

"Yes, Mrs. Geuring, uh, Grammy. Anyway, I'm trying to solve the case of who shot Billy Bollinger right down there on Route 866 just a few months ago."

"Oh, that was terrible. Nothing like that has happened out here before that I can remember."

"Did you happen to see anything Mrs. Ge..,uh, Grammy?"

"Well as it happens, I spend a lot of time sitting in my lazyboy. Here come along, I'll show you."

Grammy led Galen into the living room and next to the extremely clean window was a well worn green leather lazyboy recliner.

"This is where I spend most of my time. The light is so good and I like to read," she said.

Galen, standing next to the recliner looked out the window, across the highway and there it was, the exact spot where Billy Bollinger's car had been pushed off the road. "So Mrs. Ge......,Grammy, did you see the accident happen?"

"Well, I don't believe I would call it an accident."

"That nice shiny blue car, it was such a pretty color blue. Anyway that car ran right into that old junk heap of Billy Bollinger's and pushed it right off the highway. Then the blue car pulled in front of the other one and a good-looking man jumped out of the blue car and ran back to the old one. He was yelling, and you could tell he

16

was really mad at that Billy. You know that good-looking guy looked sort of familiar."

"Did you hear any shots, Grammy?" Galen asked.

"No, they just yelled at each other," she said, "then the good looking guy went back to his car, got in, then got back out again. I guess he forgot something. Then it looked like he hit Billy in the face and this time he went back to his car and took off in a hurry. The stones were flying and his tires were squealing when he left. It sure was a pretty blue car. Blue's my favorite color you know," Grammy said as she looked up at Chief Farr.

"Did you see anything after that?" Farr asked.

"Well sure. I hadn't had that much excitement since the kids left home, so I just kept watching."

"Did you call 911 or anything?"

"Oh no, I don't like to get involved, and it just looked like a little disagreement."

"Then what happened, Grammy?"

"Well, let's see. I need to keep these things in order." Grammy rubbed her chin while she looked out the window and appeared to be thinking. "Oh, I remember," she blurted, "that silver car was coming down the road, like from Holidaysburg? And he stopped on the other side of the road. He ran over to Billy's car."

"What happened then, Grammy?"

"Well, I had to go to the bathroom, All that excitement, I guess." Grammy blushed.

"What was the next thing you saw?" Chief Farr asked.

"Well, when I got back from the bathroom, the silver car was gone and I saw an old red pickup truck coming that same way pull off, and he ran over to Billy's car. He looked familiar too! I know I've seen him somewhere, but the old eyes just aren't what they used to be. Anyway, he ran over to Billy's car then it looked like he was talking on one of those new little phones that everyone is getting. The kind that doesn't need to be hooked to a line. I just don't understand how those things work. It's just amazing the new fangled things that people have these days..."

"Mrs. Geuring, did you hear any shots when the guy in the red pickup was there?"

Grammy rubbed her chin again, "No. No, he just talked on his new fangled phone then he was sitting in his truck till the ambulance came along. Would you like some cookies? I baked them fresh just yesterday. I have a bit of a sweet tooth, you know."

"No, thanks, Grammy. But just so I have this right, you didn't hear any shots?"

"No, I don't remember any. Of course it could have happened when I was in the bathroom. With that noisy fan on in there you can't hardly hear yourself think straight. But, then, sometimes you can't stand to be in there without the fan on," she nudged Chief Farr with her bony elbow. "Know what I mean?" she asked with a smile on her face.

"Yes, I know what you mean," Chief Farr replied.

"All tyranny needs to gain a foothold is for people of good conscience to remain silent"....Thomas Jefferson

Chapter 4

Bobby Morrow spent his time on the flight to Bonaire just relaxing, reading and watching the onboard movie, knowing that once he got on the island there would be no time for those things. Everyone gaped out the airliner windows as it made it's final approach to Flamingo Airport oohing and aaahing as the plane came in low over the sea where the locals and tourists at Windsock were enjoying the water and weather. The Caribbean Sea was the most brilliant hues of blues and greens and the expressions on everyone's face was that of sheer joy and excitement while in the back of their head some probably wondered if they needed to lift their feet to keep their toes dry. It looked like they may take the roof off the small truck passing just beneath them on the highway, and just on the other side of the highway was the beginning of the runway. The soft touchdown and short taxi to the terminal was followed by the wait while they wheeled the stairs to the door. This was not the normal modern airport where the plane pulled right up to a gateway. This was Bonaire. When the door swung open and the heat swept into the plane, Bobby knew he was here. Carrying his bag down the steps and across the tarmac to the customs and immigration area, Bobby began to relax as the sunshine combined with the tropical breeze filled with lovely smells made him relax. The only thing missing was his wife and his flowered shirt.

Bobby was able to get through customs and immigration quickly and step outside the terminal. Across the small parking lot he saw several small car rental buildings; one story concrete white buildings each displaying a different car rental company sign covering all the major companies and then a couple local companies like Island Rentals and Caribe Rent a Car. Bobby went to the Budget store and picked up a compact car making sure to get all the insurance they offered. Just in case. He had been known to return a car with bullet holes in it.

After a quick drive to the Divi Flamingo resort, he checked in, stowed his bag in his room, and immediately struck out for Wildman Clint Armstrong's place.

Bobby put the windows down in the little compact car and started down J.A.Abraham Boulevard toward downtown Kralendijk. There was no need to run the air conditioning as the tropical breeze felt just perfect. Bobby enjoyed the slow drive and turned onto Kaya Simon Bolivar then onto Kaya Korona looking for the small sidestreet and making a right turn onto Kaya Pappa Comes. There a few houses from the corner was the home of Clint Armstrong. His boat and trailer were parked across the street and his Harley Davidson bike could be seen inside the concrete wall that surrounded each home. Clint's home, like so many others here in Bonaire was a yellow stucco one story building surrounded by a yellow stucco wall with flowering shrubs sticking above the top of the wall. Bobby parked the small rental car and rang the bell at the gate. A smiling Matty came out of the home dressed in her customary flowered, flowing sarong, her long blonde hair blowing in the breeze. Any other man's heart would begin racing but Bobby was the epitome of monogamous. Matty and Bobby hugged and Matty invited him in to her home. The walls were covered with photos of fish and birds of the island as that was Matty's passion. She led Bobby out onto the covered open air patio, offered him a seat and went back into the house for two tall dripping iced teas.

"I'm sorry to hear about Clint," Bobby said.

Matty looked away then turned back with tears in her eyes, "I'm sure going to miss him."

"Can you talk about what happened, or is it too soon?" Bobby asked her.

"All I know is what the police have told me, Bobby. They said he was found on the beach. Shot." The tears were now streaming down Matty's cheeks. Bobby didn't press the issue. He knew he would get this and more from the Bonairean Police so there was no need to put Matty through anymore heartbreak.

"Is there anything I can do for you Matty?" Bobby asked in his earnest sympathetic voice.

"No, I'll be all right. Clint had some life insurance and for years he and I had talked about me opening a studio downtown so we could sell artwork to the cruise ship people."

"Sounds like a good idea."

"I already found a nice two story studio with large glass windows on the front. I repainted the outside and have it almost ready to go inside," she said, "I've needed to stay busy."

"Well you certainly have the talent."

"Yes, but most of the photos were taken when I accompanied Clint on his diving excursions. We worked really well together. So the studio is also sort of a memorial to him since it shows off a lot of his diving and all the sights he saw." Matty's faced seemed to brighten a little with the memories.

"I'm sure you'll do well Matty. Your underwater photos are spectacular and your paintings of Bonaire and the reef just can't be beat."

"Thank you Bobby. You'll have to stop by before you go back home."

"I will. I promise. In the meantime, I've kept you from your work long enough, I need to go. I just wanted to stop and pay my respects," Bobby said as he rose to leave.

Matty walked Bobby to the door and gave him a hug goodbye. While Bobby was glad that he made the effort to stop and see Matty it also reminded him that he was a few thousand miles away from his lovely wife Claire. He felt an urgency to getting to the bottom of Clint's death so he could get back home to her, so Bobby got into the dusty little compact and headed into Kralendijk to the Bonaire Police Department just off Kaya Simone Bolivar. When he arrived there, he went into the small over air conditioned office and up to the counter. There was a lady in uniform manning the counter that asked what she could do for him.

"Can I speak to the Captain, please?" Bobby asked.

22

"May I say who is inquiring?" she asked Bobby while watching him intently.

"Bobby Morrow, from the states."

The small dark Bonairean lady went to a closed door behind her, knocked gently, then entered. She came back and opened the half door so Bobby could enter, "follow me please."

Bobby followed her into the same office after she again made a quick quiet knock on the door then led Bobby in. The Captain was also a short Bonairean. Older, wrinkled from the years of exposure to the sun, with short cropped slightly graying hair and neatly dressed in his light blue uniform shirt with dark blue shorts. The shoulder patch on his shirt was the Bonairean flag with its yellow, white and blue diagonal fields, representing the sun and sea, and the compass in the corner with the word Policia under it.

"Mr. Morrow, I'm Captain Craane. How may I be of assistance?" the Captain asked while offering a firm handshake and a friendly but controlled smile.

"First Captain Craane. I am required to give you this letter of introduction from my employer," Bobby said as he handed the Captain a crisp white envelope with the White House picture and address on the upper left hand corner. The envelope was already neatly typed to the attention of Captain Craane, Bonaire Police Department. The Captain motioned for Bobby to have a seat while he returned to his seat behind his desk, sat down, and opened the envelope. After he studied the letter he looked over at Bobby, "your President would like me to consider it a personal favor to have you look into the death of Clint Armstrong," Captain Craane said slowly while intently studying Bobby.

Bobby just smiled and waited.

"Is there a particular reason that your government would be so interested in the death of a man here on our island?"

"He was a war hero, sir," was all that Bobby said.

"Must have been quite a hero for the most powerful man in the free world to take such an interest."

"Some in our country value the contributions made by our veterans, and in particular one who had received so many awards for his distinguished service as Mr. Armstrong."

"While I can appreciate that," Captain Craane went on, "the President of the United States has sent you," the Captain studied Bobby some more, "and I cannot help but wonder if there is more to his death then just a war hero dying."

Bobby took his time in answering, "not to my knowledge, Captain."

"Did you bring any firearms into our country, Mr. Morrow?"

"No. Captain, I didn't. First of all it would have been too hard to get onto the airplane, and more importantly, my President would not permit my breaking your laws. After all, I am a guest in your country."

"Well Mr. Morrow, you may have my permission to make your inquiries as long as you do not break any of our laws and that I stay completely informed about your progress."

"Thank you Captain Craane. I will be happy to let you know anything that I may find out. I would like to ask one favor of you, if I may?"

"What would that be Mr. Morrow?"

"Could I see a copy of the police report and the autopsy report?" Bobby asked.

"You may look at them here. You may not copy them or remove them. Would that be sufficient?" Captain Craane offered.

"That would be most sufficient Captain. I thank you for your assistance and I know the President thanks you as well."

With that Captain Craane spoke quietly into his phone.

Immediately the door to the Captain's office opened and the young lady came back in to escort Bobby to another even smaller office with just a desk and two chairs where he waited patiently for the information while he studied the corners of the room trying to guess where the hidden cameras may be. After a few minutes the door behind Bobby opened and the young lady laid two file folders in front of Bobby, "just come out the door when you are finished, please," she said and immediately withdrew.

Bobby opened the top folder and began reading. Clint had been found around midnight on the beach at the boatramp just of Lac Bay. His body lay on the beach on his back, next to his loaded boat. There was one gunshot to his lower abdomen. No signs of struggle. No weapons found on the deceased. He was found because an employee of the nudist colony next door thought his vehicle had been parked there an exceptionally long time after he had earlier driven by and saw Clint loading the boat. No one saw any other traffic in the area, and, naturally, there were no witnesses. Clint's watch and wallet were still on his body. His expensive diving gear appeared to all be in the boat.

Bobby next picked up the second file and read the coroner's report. Not much new there either. Clint had bled to death following a shot to the abdomen. A .38 slug had been removed that was wedged into his spinal column. No other cuts, bruises or abrasions, and there did not appear to be any self defense items like skin under his fingernails.

Bobby thought about the reports for a minute. Robbery was not a motive, and Clint obviously was not threatened by whomever approached him. But then, Clint was a big, bad dude, on an island where the locals were much smaller people. Bobby did make a mental note to check on the location where Clint's body was found; was this a normal place for Clint to go out diving or fishing. Also, was it normal for Clint to be alone or should he have been accompanied by others. After all, he was doing diving tours of the wild side. This would be the wild side, but did he normally go at night or in the daytime. Bobby knew that night diving was a big event here on the island as different fish and reef creatures came out at night like lobsters, shrimp, tarpon and a host of others. Bobby carefully closed the two reports and left the room. He handed the reports to the young lady, waited for her to confirm that they were all there then left the cool building behind and entered the heat of the day in Bonaire. Bobby's shirt was instantly damp as he fished around for his sunglasses to not only protect his eyes but to allow him to quit squinting against the brightness of the lower latitudes. Unfortunately Bobby was going to have to speak with Matty again about the location of his body and if he should have been there, plus if he should have been alone. Also, Bobby was going to need to check with the Colonel to find out a little more about Clint's undercover work and to know if his being near Lac Bay was related to that or not. So many questions, so little time.

For now, Bobby would drive out to the spot below Lac Bay and see if any clues jumped out at him. Plus lunchtime was closing in and there was a fabulous little shack at Lac Bay called Jibe City where ice cold beer and great sandwiches were always available while you watched the windsurfers hone their skills. Richard had taken Bobby and Claire there on numerous occassions as it seemed to be Richard's favorite lunch spot. Of course, Bobby remembered teasing Richard that it was Richard's favorite lunch spot because it was next to the nudist colony and occassionally they wandered out past the high wooden fence strutting their stuff in search of that all over tan with no swimsuit lines.

The drive over to Lac Bay was a fairly quick one and it felt good to let the tropical breeze blow through the car while he sped along the narrow highway being careful to look for iguanas sunning on the road or flamingos crossing the highway. The locals really frowned on turning their flamingos into roadkill.

Bobby parked in the dusty gravel parking area and made his way across the sandy patch to the bright colored wooden structure that called itself a lunch spot. The small palm limbed roof offering not only protection from the sun but sucked the tropical breeze through. The entire structure looked like it was made from driftwood and items found on the beach that had been discarded by the sea. Russell, the tall blonde, smiling, former American that owned the shack greeted Bobby with his big toothy smile and immediately asked if he would like a beer.

The story that Richard had related to Bobby was that Russell came to Bonaire with a group to dive and somehow just didn't get around to leaving.

"Sure," Bobby said, "Amstel light."

The scantily clad young girl brought the brown bottle that was dripping wet and cold to the touch.

"Would you like anything to eat?" she asked while she waited with her pencil and the small paper at the ready.

"Yeah, bring me an egg and tomato sandwich please," Bobby said, " and you may as well bring another beer." The sandwich sounded very simple, and it was, but the herbs and melted gouda cheese on the special roll made it spectacular. And being close to the equator somehow made the beer taste better.

Bobby was trying to get all the information he had so far about Wildman Clint Armstrong organized in his head but it was a task as the well built young ladies in skimpy bikinis kept flying past his field of vision showing off their windsurfing skills.

The owner, Russell, brought Bobby's sandwich over so Bobby took the opportunity to ask him if he knew Wildman Clint Armstrong. A large smile crossed Russell's face, "knew him?" he said, "he was a regular here. Everyone here knew him. Right there," Russell said while pointing to his left to an end barstool, "right there was his seat."

"What happened to him, have you heard anything?" Bobby inquired.

"Shot. Obviously by some jealous coward." Russell said, "while he was a large and imposing man, he was also the kindest, gentlest man I had ever met. And, like me, he sure loved his life here in Bonaire. He was on his boat out there every day either fishing or diving. And he would dive where few people had the balls to dive."

"Did he have any enemies?" Bobby asked.

"No. No. He was too giving to anyone he met. That's why I say it had to be jealousy. Someone jealous that a person could be that happy and enjoy life that much. Were you a friend of his?"

"Yes, we served in Vietnam together. We saw a lot of bad stuff together," Bobby answered.

"I thought I saw you here before. Have you you been?"

"Yes, my friend, Richard St.Clair and his wife, brought me and my wife here a couple years ago."

"Yes, that's it, Richard St.Clair. That is his license plate adorning our patio over there. Russell pointed to a Pennsylvania Parrothead license plate with Richards initials on it. He came here every year for a few weeks at a time, but I haven't seen him this year."

"Richard's wife, Pamela died of cancer this past year. So he has been rather down in the dumps. He is over in Aruba now, though, because Pamela stated in her will that she wanted her ashes to be spread in the Caribbean Sea."

Russell appeared to be shocked, "but Richard's wife was so young and beautiful and full of life. How can this happen?"

"It was very sudden and very sad. Richard is taking it very hard."

"He should have brought her ashes here to Bonaire, not Aruba," Russell said, " I liked them both very much. They came here for lunch a lot."

"Maybe I'll see if I can get a call to him in Aruba and see if he can come over," Bobby said.

"Yes, you should do that. It would be good for him. I will fix him one of his favorite sandwiches. You tell him the beer is on me if he comes over," Russell said and was forced to excuse himself as the girl behind the bar was calling for his assistance.

As he was walking away, he turned back to Bobby, "you, a friend of my friends Clint and Richard, you don't pay today. On the house. Thank you for coming!"

"The problem is not that people are taxed too little, the problem is that government spends too much"......Ronald Reagan

Chapter 5

Now here was a first. Richard St.Clair was standing at the check in desk at the Aruba Beach Club depressed. Such a thing should not be possible, but such was Richard's life since Pamela passed away. And especially now that he was here with her ashes to do her bidding. The lovely Aruban check-in girl sensing that something was wrong made quick work of the job at hand and handed Richard the keycard to his normal room, room 219. Richard stood there staring at the keycard for a moment as it sunk in. He was here alone. He was brought back to reality by the clanging of the happy hour bell. What the hell, he thought, may as well start drowning my sorrows. His feet moved him along without his thinking about it to the beachside bar where he climbed onto the high stool and placed his one and only bag at his feet. He again tried not to think of the bag. Sure it held his underwear and swim suits and a few shirts, but it also held Pamela's ashes. Reina, the lovely Peurto Rican girl with the long hair and great body, that managed the bar came over to greet Richard. "Mr. St.Clair, so good to have you back," she said while pulling her long hair back out of her smile, "will your wife be joining you?"

"No, I'm afraid not," was all that Richard could get out, but his face obviously told her more for she did not push the issue.

"What can I get for you Mr. St.Clair?"

"The drink with the 100 proof rum in it," Richard replied knowing he wanted to dull the pain as quickly as possible.

"The Aruban Dushi. I get that for you, Mr. St.Clair," Reina replied as she showed her dazzling bright smile and turned to make the drink. She was back in no time at all, "shall I put this on your room tab, Mr.St.Clair?"

"Yes, please," Richard said, "and Thank you."

A few drinks later and the bartender had Richard spilling his guts about Pamela and her death. The steel drum player was cranking out the island sounds, the sun was going down, the tropical breeze was blowing around the sweet fragrances of the island and Richard was actually holding a conversation.

The next morning Richard awoke, put on his swim trunks and flowered shirt, took Pamela's ashes, and went to the front desk to catch a taxi. The trip up route 1B didn't take long. But then how could it when the entire island is only 21 miles long. And, had it been for any other reason, it would have been a very pleasant drive. Mornings in Aruba with the sunshine and the brilliant blue sky were extremely enjoyable. It always felt like mother nature came at night with a giant hose and washed the island down leaving it fresh and clean.

The taxi left Richard off at the bus stop at Malmok Beach and Richard slowly meandered down to the water's edge. Richard waded into the brilliant blue water up to about his waist, thought to himself about the wonderful years he was lucky enough to have shared with Pamela, and slowly released her ashes into the current. The Caribbean Sea seemed eager to accept them. The colorful fish gathered and swam right up to Richard as though waiting for Pamela. Bright blue parrot fish, black and gold French Angelfish, numerous striped sargeant majors, bright yellow juvenile tangs, and a large orange starfish lay there marking the spot. Richard could only imagine that Pamela was now part of that gorgeous blue water. His first true love was now joined with his second love. He stood there quite a while before deciding he should wade back to the shore.

Standing on the bank was Reina, the beach bar manager from the Aruba Beach Club. She was dressed in her work outfit and had been watching Richard.

"Reina," Richard asked, "what are you doing here?"

"Pamela was a friend. You told me last night at the bar you would be here and I wanted to pay my respects so I followed you," she said, her voice barely above a whisper, "I hope you don't mind."

"No, I don't mind. Thank you for being here."

Reina reached out and touched Richard's hand, "you know that she would want you to move on. you've so much left to live for."

"I know Reina. It's just hard."

"Of course, it is. But, it will get easier."

The calm of the Caribbean Sea seemed to settle over Richard as she spoke. Reina turned to leave and said, "I will buy you a drink tonight at happy hour."

Richard thought for a moment then said, "I don't think so Reina. Thank you but I've had enough to drink to last me for quite a while. Can I buy you breakfast?"

Reina shyly looked at the ground while she shuffled her feet and replied, "I'm sorry. I have to get back to work. Perhaps another time."

"Let's ride back together then," Richard suggested and he led her up the beach to the bus stop where the bus had just deposited several tourists with their flippers and masks, beach towels and sunscreen. They rode back in silence, sitting next to each other, watching the palm trees and hotel fronts pass by until the bus made the corner at the Alahmbra Casino and deposited them near the Aruba Beach Club.

Richard walked Reina into the hotel then turned towards the steps, "thank you for being there Reina."

She smiled and went on her way to the beach bar.

When Richard got to his room, he gathered his sunscreen, his beach towel, a bottle of cold water and a book and headed for the beach. Finding a lounge chair near the water under a chickee, the palm leafed umbrella they built for shelter from the sun, he spread his towel on the chair, propped it in the semi upright position and deposited himself there. He flipped open the new paperback, "Blue Hole" by some unknown author, and began reading. The sunshine was brilliant, the blue sky fabulous, the sound of the surf was music to his ears, and the smells blowing along with the tradewinds left him know that everything was alright. He was near to dozing off and nearly dropped his paperback when he heard one of the front desk girls calling his name.

"Mr. Richard St.Clair. Mr. Richard St.Clair"

"He looked at the young lady and spoke, "I'm Richard St.Clair."

"You have urgent message at front desk Mr Richard St.Clair."

"Thank you he said. I'll be right up." Richard marked the spot in his book, gathered his towel, sunscreen, and water and followed the young lady to the check-in desk.

The lady that checked him in with the long dark hair looked at Richard and said, "I'm sorry to hear about your wife Mr. St.Clair" and she handed him the message.

Word travels fast on a small island Richard thought as he unfolded the message and read; "Richard catch a plane to Bonaire. I need your assistance. Bobby"

Richard thought for a moment, turned toward the ocean, and walked over to the beach bar.

"Reina," he said to her back.

She turned to face him, surprised by the sound of his voice.

"Richard," she said.

"I have to leave. When I come back in September, could I maybe see you?"

"I'll be waiting."

"My reading of history convinces me that most bad government results from too much government." ...Thomas Jefferson

Chapter 6

It was almost titillating to Chief Farr to be legally breaking into the house, then rummaging through every item in there. And the best part was, he could leave it a shambles and the law protected him. What made it especially exciting was the fact that it was the Mayor's house. Galen had gotten his court order and was now searching for the weapon, that he was convinced, killed Billy Bollinger. Once he found it and had it tested this case would make him a real hero not only in Ganister, Pennsylvania, but all over the state. He would show them why he should have been the Chief of Police years ago. And, ever since the mayor strode into his office looking like a drunk, swore him in, then totally disregarded his first request to an interview, Chief Farr knew payback was in order. He first rummaged through Richard's dresser drawers, then even pulled them completely out to look at the bottoms. Not because he thought a gun could actually be there, but because he was determined to leave no stone unturned. And if it left things a bit messier, so much the better. Chief Farr flipped over the mattress and box springs. He emptied everything for the bedside stand. There were 38 shells there along with an empty holster. Chief Farr's mind took off when he found that. The mayor has obviously intentionally hidden the gun if it's not in the holster. And the only reason to hide it would be because it was used in the commission of a crime. Another thought passed through the Chief's mind, "and that SOB acted holier-than-thou when he gave me time off work and made me destroy the sawed off shotgun that Chief Bollinger had given to me out of the old evidence locker. I'll show him." That gun is here somewhere and I'm going to find it. He also took time to admire Pamela's taste in underwear, as he rummaged through her drawers, at one point even taking the time to smell the cologne left on the worn bra. There were boxes under the bed that he went through. There was a lock box that he felt sure must contain the weapon, but after he busted the lock off all he found were insurance policies nd other papers. He tossed everything out of Richard's closet taking the time to go through each and every pocket. Then he did the same with Pamela's closet. Checking every pocket and at some points remembering how great she looked in some of the skimpier clothes. He tossed the couch pillows. Overturned the couch and chairs. Emptied every drawer in the kitchen, even emptied the cabinet under the sink. Pamela had some fine dishware, but not after the Chief was finished going through the china cupboard. When there was hardly a place left to walk, he moved on to the garage. He even tore apart Richard's race car looking for the gun. Another thought occurred to the Chief, "there's an empty stall here. Where is the mayor's car?" He patted his chin with his pointer finger the way he always did when he was thinking, "of course," he said to himself, "it's at the airport. I need to get another warrant and go get that vehicle. That's probably where he hid it so it wouldn't be too far away, yet not in his house just in case it got searched." The Chief left. The front door lock was broken to pieces, but, no matter this place is a wreck anyway. Galen made the call, got the warrant, and arranged to have the local flatbed towing service pick up the car. He decided he would wait in his office until the car was delivered to him. And while he waited it wouldn't hurt to have a nice cup of coffee and a few doughnuts. He even propped his feet up on the desk. What would be next for Chief Galen Farr after he cracked this case? Sheriff? State Police Commissioner?

"Man is not free unless government is limited."....Ronald Reagan

Chapter 7

Bobby was sitting on the small dock outside his room at the Divi Flamingo surrounded by the quiet of the morning as he punched the numbers into his phone. The only activity around him were the couple resort personnel at the dive shop that had just brought the white diving boat into the next pier were taking off used air tanks and replacing them with fresh air tanks to be ready for the load of divers they would be taking out to Klein Bonaire in about an hour. The clanging of the tanks was the only sound to be heard but it traveled quickly across the calm blue sea.

Bobby's phone call was answered, "Yeah?"

"Colonel," Bobby said quietly into the phone, "I need a few more details on Clint's activities here."

"There's not much I can add to our previous conversation. The drugs are coming out of South America into Bonaire and Curacao where the police departments are limited in funds and experience, then continue on to the states. We have not been successful in South America in shutting off the flow, so it seemed more advantageous to concentrate on these in between points. Clint was definitely on to something according to our last conversation but he had not given' me any names or specifics yet."

"Any idea where I can start?" Bobby asked.

"The beginning," the Colonel replied, " I knew this wouldn't be easy which is why you were selected. And most likely when you find his killer, you'll find out what he was on to."

"Can you do me favor, since I am limited on resources?"

"Shoot."

"Check on Matty's finances," Bobby said.

"No problem. I'll have the info sent to you a.s.a.p. Anything else?" the Colonel asked.

"Not unless Wildman Armstrong let you know where he stashed his notes."

"If I knew that you wouldn't be enjoying a Caribbean vacation at my expense." With that the phone went dead. Bobby was used to it, the Colonel was a man of few words, not unlike Bobby himself, so when he was done, he was done.

Bobby pressed the end button, folded his phone, and scanned the horizon. Beautiful, he thought, it's amazing how many hues of blue there can be spread out between the sky and the sea. After a few moments he meandered over to the outdoor patio where the tinkling of dishes could now be heard as they prepared the usual breakfast buffet. Fresh omelets made while you watch with whatever you wanted in them. Bobby usually had tomatoes, onions, cheese, and occassionaly some green peppers. Then after a leisurely breakfast he would take his dusty little rental car out to the airport to pick up Richard. Bobby hadn't heard from Richard, but Bobby knew when the flights from Aruba came in, and he knew Richard would be on the late morning flight. Call it psychic. Call it intuition. Whatever you call it, it showed how close these two were, so Bobby would go the airport, pick him up, then head out to Jibe City for lunch where he could get Richard up to speed on the situation.

Bobby was a little early heading to the airport, but that was a good thing. Just past the entrance to the airport the highway ran next to the beach and one of the best spots for diving and snorkeling was "Windsock". So named because there actually was a windsock flying there to show the landing planes the direction the wind was blowing. The windsock was at the edge of the beach at the highway since just on the other side of the highway was a fence enclosing the beginning of the runway. Bobby found a large chunk of coral on the beach and perched himself on it sucking up the brilliant sunshine while he scanned the ocean for signs of life and the horizon for the small dots of light that would be the airplane lights on their final approach to the runway. After seeing a few dolphins pass by bobbing in and out of the water, he saw the speck of light. The speck became larger and larger as it got closer and closer. After a few minutes Bobby was staring at the front of the dual propeller plane which didn't take long to pass directly over him. He managed to see the blue writing on the side of the plane that said Tiara Air. That would be Richard's flight so he ambled back to the car and went less than a mile to the airport parking lot and picked out a space. No use in hurrying as Richard would have to de-plane then go through immigration and customs, and when he came through the doors, Bobby would be waiting along with the others,.... well apparently there weren't many on this flight, since there weren't but a couple people waiting. There were more taxi drivers sitting at their small table playing dominoes than there were people waiting for the passengers of the Tiara Air flight.

After a few minutes the door opened and a local with a child came through the door, followed by a well dressed man overloaded with gold jewelry, then Richard. His one lone small travel bag in his left hand as he strolled over to Bobby and they shook hands and did their man hug, the old arm around the back and kind of bump pecs. Richard smiled at Bobby and said, "how'd you know I was on that flight? Pretty sure of yourself aren't ya'?"

"I know you like a book. Thanks for coming, buddy."

"So where's my chauffeur?" Richard asked.

"See the dusty old blue compact at the left end of the parking lot?" Bobby asked.

"That the best you could do?"

"It's all we need. Come on. How was your flight?"

"Bit shaky but good. It's actually nice to be on these little jitneys cause you get to see things. A lot of little fishing boats out there, and I got to see all of Curacao when we went over it. The port there had several cruise ships tucked in it and the bridge that swings was just opening when we flew over."

"You hungry?" Bobby asked.

"Well, yeah, I haven't had lunch yet."

"What have you been doing all morning?"

"I took Pamela's ashes to Malmok and spread them in the Sea just like she wanted." The mood changed quickly.

"You okay?" Bobby asked as he observed Richard's smile disappear.

"Yeah. It's been several months now. It's time to get on with things."

"Several. More like almost a year."

"Really? Guess I sort of lost track of time." Richard said.

"Well, welcome back. We got work to do."

"Where we headed?" Richard asked.

"Jibe City. Russell wanted to see you and where else are you going to get a great sandwich and cold beer cheap?"

"Jibe City. Perfect. How's old Russell doing?"

"He's like the island, nothing changes, it just putters along."

"So, what is it that is so important that I have to leave Aruba and come help you with?"

"Wildman Clint Armstrong. He took a bullet to the gut. The Colonel wants to know who and why? Clint was doing a little work for the Colonel."

"So it's probably all related. I see. And it probably means sooner or later someone is going to be shooting at us, right?"

"Well you never know, so here, you may want to keep this stashed in your swim trunks," Bobby said as he handed Richard a small Sig Sauer handgun.

"Very nice, but how do you manage to get things like this here through airport security?" Richard asked.

"Well, I don't. They just get delivered to me after I get to wherever I'm going."

"Sweet!"

"Any idea yet who we're looking for?"

"Nope."

"Any idea what whoever it is we're looking for is into?"

"Yep. The usual, running dope. Clint had his own diving operation here where he took tourists on diving trips. His was a little different though cause he took them to the wild side of the island not the usual calm side dive spots. All we know so far is the two things are related somehow."

"Have you seen Matty?"

"Yes, she seemed okay. A little broken up over losing Clint naturally, but moving on with her life. Unlike someone else I know that thought he should try to drink the world dry." Bobby shot a glance at Richard, but he wasn't looking back at him, he was looking out the dirty windshield staring into the deep blue sky. Finally Richard spoke, "well, good for her," was all he said.

The duo pulled into the dusty lot kicking up even more dust, left the windows down on the rental and mozied over to the Jibe City bar where they were warmly greeted by Russell.

"Richard St.Clair and Bobby Morrow," he bellowed, "how are my good friends?" Before they could answer he led them to a table. "Here, sit down. I'll get you a couple cold beers."

"Thanks, Russell," they said in unison.

"What I can get you for lunch today?"

Bobby said, "I want that seafood salad thing you make so well."

Richard the tamer one said, "the tomato and egg sandwich, Russell. Thank you."

"Coming right up," the gregarious Russell said as he was striding away.

As soon as they were alone Richard asked Bobby, "how are we going to get started on this thing?"

"Well, standard operating procedure for any op is to keep detailed notes," said Bobby, "so somewhere Dick had a journal or computer or something. We need to find that, then we will know what he had uncovered thus far."

"So where do we start looking for that?"

"When I visited with Matty, I asked if Clint used the computer. She laughed. She said not with the big fingers he had, so I think we're looking for handwritten notes. The question is where would he stash them. If I were him it would not be in my home. That's the first place anyone would look. I also wouldn't use a safe deposit box because, though it would be secure, it would take too many trips to it and arouse suspicion."

"So, if it's not in his house and not in a safe deposit box, what's left?"

Bobby studied the question for a moment, "well his boat seemed to be his prize possession, that's a good starting place or maybe somewhere right around us. Russell said he was here all the time for lunch."

"Dare we ask Russell?" Richard asked.

"No way. Nice a guy as he is, we just don't know who is involved in this so everyone is a suspect."

"Everyone include Matty?"

"Yes, until we exclude her. I'm working on that right now. The Colonel is pulling her financials. That should eliminate her as a suspect or move her to number one on the hit parade."

The duo hushed as the sandwiches came and were placed in front of them. Bobby smiled at the shrimp and crab leg sandwich and asked the waitress for another ice cold Amstel light. After she left the table Richard said, "so what's first?"

"First, I think we ask Matty if we can borrow Clint's boat and truck for a little diving or fishing."

The ice cold beers arrived. The bottles dripping from their introduction to the warm Caribbean heat. Out on the flat water of Lac Bay the windsurfers kept passing by. Some practicing their quick turn-arounds. A few occassionally taking the plunge into the water.

"Politics is not a bad profession. If you succeed there are many rewards, if you disgrace yourself you can always write a book."...Ronald Reagan

Chapter 8

The door opened like a tornado just came through it. The surprise caused Chief Farr to nearly fall off his chair that he had leaned back on just two legs with his feet planted on the desk.

The tow truck operator that had just come through the door bellowed at him, "where do you want this thing?"

"The Mayor's car? Out back. Just pull it into the garage."

"Who's paying for this?" the squat man with the slicked back hair asked.

"Just see the borough secretary next door. She'll write you a check," the Chief replied. Now standing and brushing the crumbs off his shirt and pants.

The Chief followed the tow truck operator out the door then headed behind the office to the garage. "Now he had him," the

Chief thought to himself, "somewhere in this car has got to be the gun."

The tow truck operator brought the car around, backed it neatly into the garage, dropped it off the hook, and wasted no time leaving for his next run. His two way radio was squawking the whole time with more potential money runs.

The Chief threw on a pair of coveralls over his nice clean uniform and started by searching under the seats, in the pockets of the seats and the doors. Then the glove compartment. At least the Mayor's car was neat and there wasn't much junk to work around. Then the Chief popped the trunk and searched in there including the spare tire well. Nothing. The Chief thought for a minute, then bounced and tugged on the rear seat until it finally gave way. Nothing there either. "Where could you possibly hide a gun in here?" he asked himself. Disgusted but figuring he just needed some time to think about it, he took off the coveralls, straightened his uniform, looked in the mirror to check his hair, and decided he would temporarily move on to his next item, searching Bobby Morrow's home for a 38 caliber handgun. Just in case. So he closed the garage door, got into the squad car and headed out to the Morrow house.

When he arrived he was amazed at how quiet it was. The log home sitting in the middle of the large field surrounded by trees on all sides. It was a picture postcard place with the brilliant green field, the log house, and the blue sky with just a couple white puffy clouds. Galen left the car, strode up onto the porch and knocked on the door. Bobby's lovely wife Claire answered the door and immediately invited him in.

"What can I do for you Chief? Bobby's not home right now," she said.

"Well, I'm sorry to have to tell you this but".......

"Bobby didn't get hurt, did he?" she interjected.

"No, Mrs. Morrow. I'm here to search your home. I have a warrant here."

"Search for what?" a confused Claire asked.

"Your husband is still a suspect in the Billy Bollinger shooting. I'm searching for the weapon."

"Well Bobby's gun cabinet is right around the corner," she pointed off to her left, "help yourself."

"Well I may have to search the entire home Mrs. Morrow."

"It won't be like in the movies where you leave a big mess everywhere, will it," she asked with a smile on her face.

"I'm not responsible for the condition afterward , only for searching every nook and cranny," he said.

The smile disappeared from Claire's face and she responded, "in that case Duke can stay with you. And if you make a mess, Duke will see that you clean it up."

"Who's Duke".....the Chief started to ask but the answer came in the form of a low growl from behind him. He turned and was staring at the largest dog he had ever seen with teeth the size of a car grill.

"Mrs. Morrow, I must warn you, if your dog attempts to bite me, I will shoot him."

"Hope you're quicker than the last guy that tried to," she said and sauntered off into the living room where the television was playing. "Watch him Duke," were her last words.

49

The Chief moved rather slowly around the corner where Claire had pointed and found the gun cabinet. It was not locked. He opened it and began picking up and examining each handgun in there. And there were quite a few. The obvious conclusion was that Bobby Morrow preferred his guns be larger than a 38 caliber. This man was a one man army with all his weapons and ammunition. Duke apparently wanted to be sure the Chief knew he was still there so he got closer to him and sniffed his crotch then growled some more. The Chief became uncomfortable again and started to sweat. Perhaps he was better off with the Mayor as his number one suspect. He carefully closed the gun cabinet door, watching Duke as he did it to be sure the dog didn't make any sudden moves.

"All done in there?" he heard Claire ask from the living room?

"Done in here but I still need to look around the rest of the house," he replied.

Carol picked up her phone and punched in the numbers that Bobby had told her to use in any kind of emergency. The phone only rang once and was answered, "Yeah?"

"This is Claire Morrow."

"Yes, Claire," the Colonel answered, "what can I do for you?"

"I think it is just awful that while my husband is out risking his life, serving his country, that this police Chief is searching our home."

"Whoa," the Colonel said, stopping her, "who is there?"

"Chief Farr of Ganister Police department."

"Hand him the phone Claire. I'll take care of this."

"Chief Farr, there's a call for you she said as she got up from the couch and went into the dining room where he was standing with Duke at his heels.

"Who's this?" Chief Farr asked when she handed him the phone.

"Chief, this is the Colonel. I work directly for the President of the United States. Mr. Morrow is in our employ. You will cease and desist from your actions or I will start with the Governor of Pennsylvania and call everyone all the way down his chain of command until your immediate supervisor makes you cease and desist. Oh that's right, your immediate supervisor would be Mayor Richard St.Clair who happens to be away tending to his wife's last wishes. I guess I'll stop at the State Attorney General and have him come in there and bust your ass. Are you hearing me Chief?" The Colonel was practically yelling by this point.

"Yes, I hear you. I just question your ability to direct my activities," the Chief said feeling confident.

"Well, I wouldn't want that," the Colonel said his voice again soft and pleasant, "just you stay right where you are and my guess is your phone will be ringing in about 3 minutes, then you won't be so cocky!" the Colonel's escalating voice as he immediately hung up. Even Claire Morrow could hear the end of his last sentence as he yelled it into the phone.

Claire stood with her hand out waiting for the Chief to give her phone back to her. The stunned Chief was moving slowly obviously in deep thought as he handed it back to her.

"Well?" Claire asked.

"I'll wait until your husband comes back and we'll continue this then," he said.

As Claire said, "fine, goodbye," Duke increased his growl and practically pushed the Chief to the door.

"Don't let the door hit you where the Good Lord split you," she said.

As soon as the door closed Duke flopped down on the floor and went back to sleep.

"One loves to possess arms, though they hope never to have occassion for them."....Thomas Jefferson

Chapter 9

Bobby and Richard left the waitress at the lunch shack at Jibe City a handsome tip, said farewell to Russell and piled into the dusty subcompact rental to head back to Kralendijk. The went up J.A.Abraham Boulevard, made the left turn onto Kaya Grandi and found themselves in front of the freshly painted Gallery of Matty Armstrong. When they entered the cool air conditioning Matty spied them and immediately hustled over to greet them. First she hugged Bobby, then spying Richard she said, "Richard, I'm so glad you have come. I'm also very sorry to hear about Pamela."
"It was quite a shock," Richard answered.
"We are in the same boat you and I."
"Yes and I'm very sorry about Clint. Hopefully Bobby can help bring some closure for you," Richard said.
"You both are very kind. It is no wonder that Clint spoke so well of you both."

"Your Gallery is lovely, Matty," Bobby said.

"Thank you. It makes me feel better to be here because with all the pictures of Clint's diving and the reef, it still seems like at least a part of him is still here," she said but with sadness in her eyes.

Richard and Bobby were impressed by the beauty that surrounded them on the walls of the Gallery.

"I came to ask a favor," Bobby said.

"Whatever you need. You are my friends."

"Could we borrow Clint's boat for a day or two to do some diving and fishing? We'll be glad to pay you." Bobby said.

Clint's boat was a thirty foot custom Zodiac dive boat that he had used to take divers to the "wild side" of Bonaire where the larger waves, steep, rocky shorelines and challenging access led to uncharted shipwrecks, pristine coral and lots of large marine life, including sharks.

"Of course, you can take it. But you cannot pay me. Clint would want you to use it. You will need to take his truck to pull it," she said, "wait here. I'll get you the keys, then you can just take it whenever you like." She disappeared into a small office and came back with the keys jingling in her fingers, "here you go. Have fun."

"Thank you so much," Richard said and Bobby concurred.

After leaving the Gallery they turned left onto Kaya L.D.Gerharts and in a couple blocks pulled into the Cultimara food store which is adorned with a colorful mural featuring local residents. They stocked up on water, beer, sandwiches and some ice for the cooler then headed off to pick up the boat.

Clint was obviously a neat freak. Everything was clean and shiny on the boat and the truck.

"Try to remember," Richard said to Bobby, "this isn't your beat up old Chevy. Some people actually take care of their equipment."

"So do I," said Bobby.

"Like what?" Richard asked.

"You ever see one of my guns dirty?"

"Well you got me there. It's just that your vehicles leave a lot to be desired."

"Priorities, Richard. Priorities. Now get the cooler loaded and let's get this show on the road."

The duo pulled out onto Kaya Simon Bolivar and wound around the stadium onto Kaya Internashional which would take them out past the airport, past Windsock and Pink Beach. Past the salt works where the flamingos were busy shifting their heads in the water from side to side searching for food, and at the same time getting the bonus of more pink for their feathers. Around the curve at the southern end of Bonaire and up the other side until just before Lac Bay where they took a small road. If you could actually call it a road as it was more like a trail, directly out to the edge of the ocean at the one spot where the banks were jagged lava and coral but where mother nature had provided a narrow sand sloped bottom and enough water to get in the boat before the waves and the current caught you. Before they unloaded the boat they took the time to casually search through the truck including under the dash looking for Clint's journal or notes. Nothing in the truck so while they still had daylight and no one was around to watch them they began searching the boat. They looked in all the compartments and especially any that were locked. They looked under the dash, under the motor cover, everywhere they could think of. They were close to giving up and sat down on the side benches to think and discuss where might be left to search.

"We've looked everywhere but in these air tanks," Richard said.

"Yeah, but they're full of air. Aren't they?" Bobby asked. The two immediately checked the valve on each bottle of air. Only one was empty, the rest were full.

"How do you hide something in an air tank?" Richard asked.

Bobby didn't know but if it was there he was going to find out. He started twisting, pulling and turning everything he could. then exasperated he slammed it down. "It's not in there," he said.

Richard placed the bottle back where it originally was and strapped it back into place. The strap kept the bottles from falling when the seas were rough. You sure wouldn't want the gauge to get broken off cause the airtank would become a missile then. Most boats just used bungi cords to tie down the tanks, but Clint had a nice black strap with velcro to hold his in place which were fastened right into the boat so they wouldn't get lost like the bunji cords. Richard didn't get the velcro strap tightened properly so when Bobby hit the throttle the empty bottle busted loose and rolled back to the back of the boat. Richard grabbed it before it went overboard and struggled to refasten it as the boat surged out through the line of breakers into the swells of the sea. As Richard worked with the strap he found it had a very fine zipper running along the back. He unzipped it and found Clint's notes.

"When you get to a calm area Bobby, you might want to take a look at this" he said as he held up the notes.

"What do they say?" Bobby asked.

"Beats me. It's some kind of shorthand or something. You'll have to look them over."

"Here, you take the wheel while I look at them before we lose what little light we have."

The sun was rapidly dropping into that little seam where the sky meets the water and where doubt rises as to whether the earth really is flat and that it's the edge of our world.

Richard eased off the throttle and let the boat come to a stop after they had gotten out to a point where the lights of Jibe City and the nudist colony were just barely visible. Bobby was using a small flashlight to look over the notes. After a moment he said to Richard, "where does the GPS say that we are?"

Richard read off the numbers to Bobby.

"Keep going straight out until until the last number gets to 15," Bobby said.

"So you found something in Clint's notes?" Richard asked.

"Something, I just don't know what. But whatever it is it's at 12 degrees 10' North 68 degrees 15' West."

With that Richard hit the throttle and the nimble little boat shot forward into the now relatively calm waters of the Caribbean Sea. After just a few minutes Richard brought the boat to a halt again, "We're here. Wherever here is."

"Okay," Bobby said, "suit up, we're going in."

"Excuse me, but, in case you haven't noticed it's dark as hell in there. Not to mention there are sharks in there looking for their nighttime snack."

"Stop complaining and put on the wetsuit. You're a tough guy. You can handle a little shark."

"But I don't even like diving. I'm a snorkeler."

"The only difference is you'll be under the water. Let's go. Oh, by the way, guess what the name of this spot is."

"What, shark city?"

"Believe it or not, it's Blue Hole."

"You're puttin' me on. Like our Blue Hole back home where I learned to swim and stuff?"

"Yeah. Blue Hole. Let's go."

The two pulled on the wetsuits that Clint kept stowed on board, put on their belts, tanks, and flippers, and strapped the big underwater lights onto their wrists then backwards over the side of the boat they went. They swam down to about 100 feet and with the darkness did not notice the shipwreck until they were just a few feet from it. The strong underwater lights providing great light but at a minimum range in the deep black water. Richard was studying the opening along a portion of the side when he felt something near him. With his periferal vision he could see Bobby's light moving back and forth just off to his left. When he swung his light to the right there was the huge eyeball of the monster fish just a couple feet to his right, looking right at him.

"We are never defeated unless we give up on God."...Ronald Reagan

Chapter 10

Chief Galen Farr came into his office, threw the car keys on the desk and assumed his position. The cup of steaming hot coffee near his right elbow, his feet crossed on the desktop, and the chair rocked back onto the back two legs. Then, after some scrutiny, he picked a doughnut out of the box, studied it some more, and took a bite. Now it was time to get down to business. The business of the Billy Bollinger murder case.

The Mayor is still a great suspect, but finding his gun would be key. The Mayor was definitely at the scene. The Mayor admits to putting his pistol to Billy's head. And he had motive. Billy had assaulted Richard's wife while they were in Aruba. Plus there was the incident, that Galen did not know all the details about, where the Mayor, former Chief of Police Bollinger and Billy were at the Blue Hole. From what Galen heard then Chief Bollinger had lured the Mayor to the Blue Hole with the aim of drowning him there. Somehow Bobby Morrow and Carmine Rizzo, the local mafia head

came to the Mayor's rescue. It was right after that that Chief
Bollinger was interrogated for the murder of the pizza man and not
much later the Chief was shot after breaking into the Mayor's
house with the intent of shooting the Mayor because the Chief was
sure the Mayor had shot his son Billy. Ganister was becoming a
little Peyton Place. Now, it was up to Chief Farr to get this murder
solved and this whole mess behind them so the sleepy little town of
Ganister can go back to being a sleepy little town. A place where
the Chief can kick back and enjoy his morning doughnuts.

Getting back to his thoughts, Chief Farr went on to his second
suspect. That of Bobby Morrow. Bobby more than likely had a 38
pistol. After all, he owned every other type of gun. Just because the
Chief hadn't found it, didn't mean it didn't exist. And Bobby had
great motive for shooting Billy Bollinger too, because Galen had
worked on that case at the time, where Billy Bollinger had raped
Bobby Morrow's daughter. Even the Mayor, at the time, was
worried that Bobby would take matters into his own hands and
shoot Billy. Maybe he just waited for a more opportune time. And
since the man everyone thought was a nice friendly dentist turned
out to be an undercover federal agent, he probably had the skills to
easily get rid of the weapon and eliminate any traces of his own
involvement. Plus Chief Farr's one eyewitness, which no one knew
about yet except Galen, saw both the Mayor and Bobby at the
scene of the crime. So, at least they could be placed there. The only
question is who shot him.

The only other potential is the silver car that Grammy Geuring saw
at the scene. But silver is the most popular color for cars and she
did not know a make or model. That was like looking for a needle

in a haystack. In Ganister alone there probably were a hundred silver cars.

Galen rooted through the remaining doughnuts. Grabbed the chocolate one with the icing on it and resumed his thoughts. As soon as those two, The Mayor and Bobby Morrow got back to town, he was just going to have to haul them in here and get down to some serious questioning. He could break them. They weren't as bright as they thought they were. And then he'd get the gun that shot Billy and wrap this case up in a nice neat bow.

Hum, that chocolate doughnut was pretty good, Galen reached for the box for another but came up with an empty box. Surprised he lurched just a little and the weight shifted on the back two legs of the chair and down he went. Crash. Galen and the chair were stretched out on the floor. He jumped up as fast as he could and looked around the empty office to be sure no one could have captured his fall.

"I predict future happiness for Americans if they can prevent the government from wasting the labors of the people under the pretense of taking care of them".....Thomas Jefferson

Chapter 11

Richard worked his flippers as fast as he could to come to a complete stop in the water all the while keeping the light drilled on the huge black eyeball of the humongous gray shape next to him and wishing he could shout out to Bobby to save himself before it was too late. Then it happened, a slap on his left shoulder. *"No he thought, there are more than one. I'm going to be eaten by sharks and will never see the light of day again."* Richard's life began to flash before his eyes. His thought of the Blue Hole that he cherished in Ganister and how ironic it was that his life ended here in the Blue Hole in Bonaire. Again this time harder the slap on his left shoulder. He wheeled around with the light determined to go down fighting and strike back at his attacker. He nearly knocked Bobby's mask off his face. Then he gathered himself and saw Bobby motioning to go up. Richard didn't need any more encouragement to swim as fast as he could to save his life, hoping

Bobby could keep up to him and save his life also. Richard shot through the surface, took a rapid look around and swam as fast as possible across the top of the water to the waiting boat. As soon as he could touch it he launched himself into the boat before any sharks could take off his legs. But then, there was nothing. *"Where was Bobby?"* he wondered. *"The sharks must have gotten my best friend. I should have stayed with him and helped him fight them off."* Just as he was preparing to put his mask on and go back in he saw Bobby break through the surface and slowly make his way to the boat.

"Hurry up," he yelled at Bobby.

"Why? What's the hurry?" Bobby asked.

"There was a shark next to me."

Bobby started to laugh, " that was a tarpon, you idiot. He was just using your light to find a meal." More laughing. "Is that what made you swim like you were in the Olympics?"

"Just come on. Get your ass on the boat before I leave without you."

Bobby was still laughing when he climbed onboard the boat. He looked at the disgusted Richard and said, "great night for a dive isn't it?"

"Oh kiss my..."

Bobby laughed some more.

"So now that we wasted an evening, let's get back to shore," Richard said.

"We didn't waste anything," Bobby said as he smiled and shook a small container in front of him. "I found Dick's notes. Right where he said they would be."

"You're putting me on."

"Get a flashlight. Let's see what's in here," Bobby said as he began unscrewing the lid on the waterproof container which had been taped to the inside of the wreck.

Richard came with the light. Bobby shook the paper out of the container and they both read it. When they were done they just looked at each other.

"That sounds like science fiction to me," Richard said.

"Sounds to me like the bad guys have been studying our navy."

"So what do we do?" Richard asked.

Bobby looked at his watch, then back at Richard, "we wait."

"Government is like a baby. An alimentary canal with a big
appetite at one end and no sense of responsibility at the
other."......Ronald Reagan

Chapter 12

Richard and Bobby waited. The boat bobbed in the relatively calm,
dark Caribbean Sea while they waited. Bobby watching the waves
out toward the horizon. Richard watching the tiny lights at Jibe
City wishing he were there sucking down an ice cold Amstel Light
and eating a fresh homemade Caribbean sandwich. He turned to
check on Bobby and just past Bobby in the water, he saw it.
"Look!" he yelled at Bobby, "Look there! I told you there was a
shark down there.
Bobby spied the dorsal fin an just shook his head. Then another
showed up. Up and down the water they went. A string of dorsal
fins up and down in the water as the column progressed.
"They are dolphins," Bobby finally said to Richard. "somehow we
have to get a good look at them."

Bobby began pulling on his airtanks again along with his mask and flippers. "You wait here, while I check this out," Bobby said to Richard. And off the side of the boat he went.

Richard just shook his head. He was convinced that his best friend was going to get eaten by a shark. Richard watched Bobby's light sway back and forth in the water as he swam toward the column of dorsal fins. Richard could tell he was right amongst them when he saw the underwater light turn around and head back to the boat. When the underwater light reached the boat it went out and Bobby reached up and grabbed the side of the boat. He pulled off his mask and said to Richard, " I'm going to follow them."

"What's going on?" Richard asked.

"I'll tell you later, you take the boat into shore, then quietly and without being spied, walk down the beach until I signal you," Bobby replied then pulled on his mask and was back under the water. His underwater light again heading to the column of dorsal fins which he joined and swam along with them toward the shore at an angle from where the boat was sitting. The dolphins had a strap around their neck, similar to a bungi cord with a package at the bottom about the size of a brick. It was an easy swim for Bobby as he grabbed onto the dorsal fin of a passing dolphin and let the dolphin pull him along. When they reached the shore Bobby let go and stood on the top of a large brain coral where he was able to have just his head out of the water. He took off his mask so he could observe. There was a concrete canal that made it's way from the sea into the building. It was just like the canal at the Sonesta Hotel in Aruba. There the canal went into the Sonesta Hotel's lobby where they loaded their guests into small boats to ferry them out to their private island where they could sun and swim. Here the canal was wide enough for dolphins to swim in and out at the same time. The walls were concrete and ended in the center of the building in a circular pool. The dolphins would swim in to where a man stood in the center of the pool. He would pull the strap with the package from around their neck and toss it to another man up on the floor. The man in the water would then give the dolphin a fish reward and the dolphin would swim around the circular pool and back out the canal into the dark Caribbean Sea. Bobby stood and watched the procession a while before donning his mask and swimming up the beach a ways.

Richard, knowing Bobby had a plan, did as he was told. He started the boat and cruised into the beach. Finding the particular sandy area was a little bit of a challenge in the dark but after a few minutes he located it. Then he had to gun the motor to get through the last line of breakers and up onto the sandy beach where he jumped out quickly with the rope in one hand and hauled the boat up onto the shore. He pulled it up out of the water as far as he could then tied it off to the trailer that was hooked to Wildman's truck. When he was sure it wouldn't go anywhere, even if the tide came in, he took off the wetsuit, stashed it in the truck, pulled on a dark windbreaker, made sure he had his gun and a flashlight and carefully made his way down the coral beach. Richard was glad he had his water shoes on as the coral underfoot was nothing like sand. It was actually part coral, part volcanic lava all mixed together and forming a pock-marked moon-like surface that was very hard to walk on. The starlight didn't provide as much light as

Richard would have liked, which slowed him down, but, given Bobby's instructions, he didn't want to use the flashlight unless he absolutely had to. So he took his time and silently cursed every time his toe caught in a coral hole. He was along the water's edge and a structure of some sort was just coming into view when he saw the quick flash of Bobby's light from the water. Richard made his way a little further down the beach and met up with Bobby who had just climbed out of the water.

"What is that building?" Bobby asked Richard in a hushed tone. Richard whispered back, "that would be the old shrimp farm. It's been closed down since right after it opened. Someone thought they could raise shrimp here and become a millionaire. Didn't work out. So what's going on, Bobby?"

"They are using trained dolphins. They strap the bags of drugs on them and the dolphins take them from point A to point B. Point B happens to be here. There is a small canal that runs right into the building. The dolphins swim into the building where they unstrap the packages and send the dolphins back out again."

"Are you serious?"

"Our Navy has been experimenting with this for a longtime, getting dolphins to deliver bombs. Apparently the drug lords have stumbled onto the technology. It's perfect."

"So this is what Dick found out that got him shot?"

"No doubt, but there still is the question of how did someone walk right up to Dick and shoot him without Dick showing any signs of defense?"

"Were you able to make out anyone inside the building?"

"Yes," Bobby said in his hushed tone, "but let's get back up the beach where we can talk without getting shot."

The duo cautiously made their way back to the boat and the truck.

"Let's get the boat loaded and head out of here," Bobby said.

They kept the lights off on the truck while they backed it down to the water's edge and as quietly as possible loaded the boat, strapped it down, and headed out to the highway with their headlights off. They took the shortcut back to Kralendijk and managed to find parking on the street at the back entrance to the resort. The resort was quiet at this time of night since the majority of the guests were divers and would be getting up early for their first morning dive. The beach bar was closed so the duo went to their room where they could continue their conversation.

"All tyranny needs to gain a foothold is for people of good conscience to remain silent."…..Thomas Jefferson

Chapter 13

"Come on man, get the hell out of bed," Bobby was saying to Richard while shaking him, "it's almost lunch time. You're going to sleep the whole day away."

A drousy Richard rolled over and stared at Bobby, "we were out half the night and yesterday was a long day for me. Not to mention you scared the hell out of me with that night diving. Are you sure that was a tarpon and not a shark?"

"Yes, I'm sure now come on, we got work to do."

"All right. All right. I'll meet you at the pool in a few minutes. I need a quick shower."

Bobby left the room while Richard trudged off to the shower. When Richard left the room he found Bobby at the pool chatting with Bob and Betty, timeshare owners from Pennsylvania that Richard had introduced Bobby to the last time they were here, along with their wives, which caused Richard to flash back in his mind. The good old days.

"It's about time. I was justing asking Bob and Betty if they wanted to join us for lunch at City Cafe," Bobby said to Richard.

"Great, can you join us?" Richard asked.

"Not this time," Betty said, "we just got back from shopping downtown. We're going to be by the pool for a little bit."

"Well we'll talk to you later then," Bobby said as the two of them headed for the back gate of the resort and made their way downtown.

City Cafe was on Kaya Craane just a short walk from the resort and situated across the narrow street from the harbor. It was a great place to sit, eat, and watch the ships come and go. Occassionally you could watch more than that. Once when Richard and Pamela were there they saw a large marlin dancing on his tail out in the water. It turned out that a local fisherman standing on the pier had caught him with his spool of fishing line and was slowly hauling him into shore. It created enough excitement that a large group gathered on the pier, including Richard and Pamela, to watch the spectacle. The Bonairean had nearly gotten the fish to the pier when a large freighter came into the harbor to dock at the pier. The Harbormaster, being one of the spectators, and a friend of the Bonairean fisherman went out on his boat and forced the freighter to stop while the fisherman hauled his catch in. The fisherman proudly held the large fish by the spear while people took photographs. He was a happy Bonairean and the visitors were extremely impressed at the crude fishing technique involving only a spool of fishing line. No rod. No reel. Just bare hands wrapping the sharp line around the spool while the large fish fought to get away.

Richard and Bobby ordered burgers and were drinking cold Amstel Lights when Richard stood up from the table. "Hey Bobby. There's Matty. We should go say Hello to her."

Bobby looked in the direction Richard was looking and yanked him down in his chair, "Shhhh. Pretend you don't see her."

"But, why? What's going on?" Richard quietly asked.

"She's with someone," Bobby quietly answered.

"So?"

"That guy was in the old shrimp plant last night. He was the one standing on the floor that the other guy threw the packages to."

"No kidding?" Richard asked as he snuck another peek.

"Now we have a real problem," Bobby continued whispering quietly to Richard, "is Matty in on this thing? And if this guy knows Matty, did he also know Clint?"

"All good questions," Richard said, "but what we need are answers."

"I already have a call in to the Colonel to have him check on Matty's financial status. I guess I better get that info quick. And we need to find out who this guy is."

"I think I can get a photo with my camera if you hold the newspaper up a little. Then we can email the photo to the Colonel."

"Good idea," said Bobby as he held up the newspaper, "how's this?"

Richard flipped open his phone, pushed a few buttons and said, "Okay, got it."

"Good, let's get out of here before we're spotted," said Bobby.

"But we didn't eat yet," protested Richard.

"Catch the waitress. Tell her to make it to go and wait over at the crowded bar. I'll be outside." Bobby got up leaving no room for discussion and slipped out of the restaurant.

Richard stood at the bar with dozens of other people all waiting for food to go and kept watch on the couple. When the waitress brought his boxes of food, Richard paid and left as inconspicuously as possible.

He found Bobby across the street behind the fruit stand sitting on the wall with his feet dangling over but not able to reach the water. "Here you go, buddy," Richard said as he handed him a box, "cheeseburger in paradise."

"That it is my friend."

The two ate while looking out across the water. Each lost in thought. Both thinking of women. Bobby thinking of his wife, Claire, and wanting to get back home to her. Richard of his former wife, Pamela, and hoping she would be at peace now that he spread her ashes in the Caribbean Sea just as she wished. When the burgers were gone, they looked at each other, and not needing to say anything got to their feet.

"I think we should call the Colonel, then go over to the police station and see Captain Craane," Bobby said.

"Should we go back for the car?"

"No, the police station is walking distance from here. Let me call the Colonel first." Bobby flipped open his cell phone and hit the speed dial number for the Colonel.

"Yes, Bobby," came the Colonel's quick answer to the phone.

"Richard is going to email you a picture. We need to know who he is, if possible. Also, have you had a chance to check on Matty Armstrong's financial status?"

"Yes, I have. Seems she has come into some money recently."

"Do you think she may be involved?"

"That's what you need to find out. Send me the photo." And, as usual the phone line went dead.

"Send him the photo Richard. He's waiting," Bobby said to Richard, "and our friend Matty has come into some money."

"You mean she may be involved in her husband's death?"

"We have to assume that until we find out differently," Bobby replied.

"That's going to make it hard even talking with her.."

"Yeah, well, that's why we get the big bucks. You cannot let on to her. We have to appear naive about her finances while we check on her possible involvement."

"Oh sure no problem. I'll just say thanks for the use of Clint's boat while we use it to try and prove you murdered him," Richard said, knowing that that was exactly what they had to do.

"Let's go see Captain Craane," Bobby said.

"Lead the way."

Bobby and Richard walked the few blocks over to the police station. Entered, and asked to see Captain Craane. The young Bonairean lady in the uniform didn't say a word to them just turned and went into the Captain's office. She came back out again followed by the Captain.

"Ah, Mr Morrow. Please, come into my office," the Captain said then opened the half door at the counter and let them enter. Bobby followed by Richard walked into the Captain's office and stood while the Captain went around his desk and sat down.

"Please Mr. Morrow, have a seat. And whom is your friend?'

"Yes, Captain Craane, this is Richard St.Clair, a friend from the states. He is Mayor of the town we live in."

The Captain rose from his seat and held out his hand, "so nice to meet you, Mayor St.Clair." The Captain then sat again and looked to Bobby, "so Mr. Morrow, is there something I can do for you?"

"Actually, Captain, I believe it's my turn to do something for you."

The Captain's eyebrows raised, "Really?"

"We have discovered what Clint Armstrong discovered that probably cost him his life."

"Really?" the Captain asked again.

"We have found a source of drugs entering your lovely island. I will give you all the information very soon. I am checking on an identity that will be of immense help to you and we still need to find out how often this occurs or if there is a particular schedule."

"Can you not tell me anything more now?" the Captain asked.

"Well, I could, but I would prefer that only the three of us know anything at this point. No offense but this is a small island. I don't know who knows who. You understand, I hope?"

"I do. And I appreciate you keeping me in the loop. Have you come any closer to finding out who shot your friend? After all, that is why you are here, correct?"

"Yes sir, that is why we are here. The other thing is just something we have come across, and we will be giving you all the information on that so that you can make the necessary arrests," Bobby said.

With that the Captain rose, letting it be known that the meeting had come to an end. Richard and Bobby rose and headed for the door.

"Oh Captain, one more thing," Bobby said, "is there a private number that we could call you at when we get information?"

"Of course, Mr. Morrow, please feel free to call me at 717-8000."

"Thank you, Captain Craane."

As the duo left the Police station, Richard quietly asked Bobby, "do you really want the Captain's phone number?"

"Sure. Hold that thought," Bobby said. Bobby opened his cell phone and pressed the speed dial button. When it was picked up he said, "Colonel, after you find out who the person in the picture is, perhaps you'll get his phone records. Then cross reference for any calls to Matty Armstrong and this number, 717-8000."

There was a minute while Bobby listened, then, "thank you Colonel." Bobby closed his phone looked at Richard, "we have got to get this finished. I want to go home and be with Claire, and I'm sure you have something better to do. Right?"

Richard looked at Bobby then replied, "yes, I get to have my Chief of Police interrogate me about a shooting I didn't do."

"Well join the club. The Colonel and Claire both told me he was at my house with a warrant looking for a gun. A 38 special. You know, like the one you tossed in the Blue Hole?"

"Yes, I tossed it in the Blue Hole, but for the last time I'm telling you, I did not shoot him."

"Well he was dead when I got there. So, if you didn't do it, then someone came after you and before me. So, when we get back, we have to find out who that someone was, otherwise one of us is going to be sitting in the pokey."

"Yeah, well, more importantly, you do believe me that I didn't do it?" Richard asked Bobby.

"I believe you, you just do stupid things to make yourself look guilty."

"Like what? Tossing the gun?"

"Yeah, like tossing the gun. For a smart guy you do some dumb stuff."

Bobby looked at Richard and paused before he went on, "I'm sorry I couldn't be with you in Aruba when you spread Pamela's ashes in the Sea."

"I didn't ask because I thought it was something I should do by myself. You know, a little private time between me and Pamela."

"Yeah, I understand."

"I miss her Bobby. But letting go of her ashes seems like she's saying to me, 'get on with your life.' Know what I mean?"

"I do. And she would be right. You have to get on with your life."

"I am," Richard said, "I'm here helping you, then I'm going back to Ganister and get on with my life. I'll miss her and I'll always love her, but I will get on with the rest of my life."

"Good man," Bobby said as he punched Richard in the arm, "now. Let's get this thing over with and catch that big bird back to the states."

The two had walked nearly back to the resort when Bobby's phone rang. He answered it, "Colonel."

"I see," Bobby said, "thanks." Then he hung up.

"The man in the photo from the old shrimp plant, his name is Cordell Sherrod."

"Name doesn't mean anything to me. Should it?"

"Maybe not. But, he happens to be a Venezuelan drug kingpin."

"Great. And Matty is keeping company with him."

"Not only that but the money that has flowed into Matty's account recently came from his account."

"Now what?"

"Now, we get the car and pay Matty a visit. Let's roll."

"Government's first duty is to protect the people, not run their lives."....Ronald Reagan.

Chapter 14

ROY G. BIV. The acronym that describes the colors of the rainbow (red, orange, yellow, green, blue, indigo, and violet) paled in comparison to the walls in Matty's gallery. As soon as you walked through the doors of the downtown Kralendijk gallery your senses were assaulted by an enormous array of colors filling every inch of wall space depicting Matty's paintings and photos of fish and marine life. The vivid colors that they wear in nature were portrayed in her paintings, from bright blue and green parrot fish to the awesome blues and yellows of the Queen Angelfish, the brilliant pink of the Squirrelfish, and even the brown and white combination of the Drum. Not to mention the tremendous assortment of marine life whose color changes constantly. Then there is the underwater backgrounds of colorful corals, sponges and sea fans.

Standing in the doorway of Matty's gallery, which she named in memory of her recently deceased husband, Wildman Gallery, was like walking into the Sea after Moses parted it. On all sides of you were beautiful fish and marine life.

Richard stopped just inside the doorway and took pause. Besides being so full of color, the paintings were so real to life. The fish were exactly as he saw them when he snorkeled. Though the gallery was full of guests, Matty caught Richard's arrival and made her way over to greet him. She was the same vivacious person she had always been and looked simple but ravishing in her light blue sundress with her blonde hair blowing back as she crossed the room. She immediately gave Richard a hug and quick kiss on the cheek.

"Richard so good to see you again."

"Thank you, Matty. I really wanted to spend some more time in your lovely gallery, and, we do need to talk privately when you can," Richard said.

"We had a cruise ship dock this morning so there are a few visitors at the moment but they will clear out very soon. In the meantime, would you like a cup of tea?"

"Yes, that would be great."

"Come," she told Richard as she led the way to the back corner of the gallery and through a small archway into the work area. The water was already hot so she poured two cups and placed the tea bags in to soak.

"First of all, allow me to again Thank you for the use of Clint's boat," Richard said.

"Has it been helpful?" she asked.

"Yes, very."

Matty's smile faded and she became misty eyed as she asked, "have you found out who shot my husband?"

"Not yet. Bobby is making progress but we don't know yet."

The bell on the door rang again so Matty got up from her chair and peeked through the archway.

"Just the guests leaving," she said to Richard and made her way back to sit down again.

"So what did you want to talk to me about, Richard?"

"You realize that every inquiry is not done to find a guilty person. Some inquiries are done to remove any doubt about an innocent person."

"Yes..." she said suspiciously.

"So I have to ask you about this," Richard said as he motioned with his hands the gallery around him, "and in particular where the money came from."

"So because I received money I am a suspect in my own husband's murder?" she asked coolly.

"Well Bobby and I would prefer that you look at it differently. We want to remove any doubt by anyone regarding yourself, so we can narrow the field down and get to the guilty person quicker."

"I see your position as mayor has become ingrained in you. You speak like a politician."

"Hopefully not like a politician with a forked tongue. My friend, Gary always says to me, 'how do you know when a politician is lying? His lips are moving.' But I would like to think that I can be an exception to that."

Matty sat motionless as Richard went on, " Bobby and I think the world of you. And Clint was one of Bobby's best friends, so this is very personal to both of us. We want whoever shot Clint to pay. Dearly. And we won't rest until that is accomplished."

"Well, I will tell you that I am coming into some life insurance money from Clint. But I have not yet received that. And frankly, when I do, I will need it to live on. As you can imagine, we needed both incomes to live. Now there is only mine, and it is up and down like a rollercoaster depending on the cruise ships and the economy and everything else that influences a person's decision to pay for art," Matty paused to collect her thoughts, "I was only able to open the gallery because a Venezuelan businessman offered to back me because he liked my paintings."

"And that would be Mr Sherrod?" Richard asked.

Matty looked at Richard strangely and asked, "yes, how do you know that?"

"How well do you know Mr. Sherrod, Matty?"

"Not very. I only recently met him."

"Did he know Clint?"

Jean thought a moment, "I don't think so. In fact, I believe the first time I met him he was actually looking for Clint. Something about diving on the wild side. Then when he came into our house and saw my paintings and photographs, he said that I should have a gallery."

"So when did you actually get the money from him?" Richard asked.

Matty gave Richard the suspicious look again and said, "very soon after Clint's funeral, but, why do I think you may already know that?"

"You're right. We know the date. And I 'm sorry to have to be so blunt but, the question is how well did you know him prior to Clint's death?"

"You surely don't think that the money had anything to do with Clint's death? Can you?" she asked, standing, hands on hips, glaring at Richard like he had the plague.

"Tell me. Straight up Matty. When did you become friends with Mr. Sherrod?"

"Like I told you," her voice rising, "I met him shortly before when he was looking for Clint. Then shortly after Clint's funeral he offered to loan me the money to open the gallery."

"Loan? So you have a written document?" Richard asked.

"Yes!" she said defiantly, "and I will show it to you." She moved around Richard to her desk. Pulled open a drawer, ruffled through a few papers, and held the document out to Richard to inspect. "Are you happy now?" she asked in her nastiest tone.

"Matty....." Richard was temporarily at a loss for words, "Matty, what do you know about Mr. Sherrod?"

"I know that he is, obviously, a successful businessman in Venezuela. What more do I need to know. My attorney's wrote the document. It is a loan. I pay interest. What are you getting at, Richard? And where is Bobby, anyway?"

"Bobby is out looking for Mr. Sherrod."

The silence was immediate and frightening until Matty finally spoke, "why, Richard?"

"Matty, Mr. Sherrod is a drug kingpin in Venezuela. He may have loaned you money to launder it. And further more, he may be involved in Clint's death. There. I've said it. It's out there. And I'm sorry to drop it on you like this but this is not a time to speak like a politician." As soon as Richard finished, he moved towards Matty and hugged her. He held her and comforted her as he knew it would not take long for the words to sink in. All the hurt of losing her husband would soon be rushing right back in. Richard knew this well because it wasn't that long ago that he lost his beautiful partner and wife, Pamela. So Richard held her. At first there was no response then he could feel her arms encircle him and her chest began to heave with the silent sobs that soon turned into the flooding tears of a woman in love that had lost her husband.

It took awhile for Matty to compose herself. When she did she reached for a tissue. Dried her eyes, blew her nose, and quietly asked Richard, " do you think Sherrod killed my Wildman?"

"We think he is a good suspect. And now that you have told me he came to your place looking for Clint, I think he is an even bigger suspect."

Jean stood quietly for a moment, then said, "please find out for sure. If he did, I want to know. I will kill that bastard myself if I find out he shot my Clint."

The preceeding outpouring of emotions had prevented Matty and Richard from hearing the tinkling of the bell attached to the door when the patron had entered. But hearing the crying and the conversation the patron had made his way back to the doorway and had quietly observed Richard and Matty. The conversation having died down, the patron joined Richard and Matty in the small workroom. He cleared his throat to get their attention.

"Sherrod." Richard said as he turned to face the intruder.

"I seem to be at a disadvantage. You know my name, but I don't know yours."

"St.Clair. Richard St.Clair. What can we do for you?"

"Oh just checking on my investment."

"Could you please leave." Matty said not any too politely.

"Yes, I think I shall. But I think you two will come with me."

"Don't bet on that," Richard said as he took a step towards Sherrod.

Sherrod smoothly produced a small gun, stepped around Richard, grabbed Matty by the arm and placed the gun against her head, "okay, Richard St.Clair, your move. Would you like to join us or shall I just shoot her here?"

"Shoot her and I'll kill you with my bare hands before you can ever get off a second shot."

"Shall we find out or would you rather lead the way out to my car out front?"

Richard didn't have to think too long. He turned on his heel, and slowly made his way to the front door of the gallery. Opening it he saw the black Lincoln with the driver leaning against the fender waiting. Matty struggled to free her arm to no avail and finally followed Richard. The driver opened the rear door and Richard slid in followed by Matty and Cordell Sherrod. The driver jumped in and with the tires squealing made his way down Kaya Grande street and made a quick right turn onto Kaya Gerharts heading out of downtown towards the airport.

"When the people fear the government, there is tyranny. When the government fears the people, there is liberty."....Thomas Jefferson

Chapter 15

Bobby Morrow could hardly hear his phone ring with the horns blasting from the cruise ship as it got underway to leave the port in Bonaire.

"Bobby," was all the Colonel on the other end said.

"Yes, Colonel," Bobby answered so he could be just as efficient.

"There does not appear to be any connection between Captain Craane and Cordell Sherrod. You may feel free to clue him in on what you know so far since it is his turf."

"Thank you, Colonel."

"Wrap this up immediately, Bobby!"

"Yes, Sir!" Bobby said but no one heard him except line static.

Bobby debated for a minute, should he call or visit the Captain. The beautiful sunny day beckoned so he left the resort, jumped in his compact rental car and headed downtown.

Bobby no sooner entered the Police Station when the same Bonairean lady in uniform, after seeing who just came in, immediately went to the Captain's office and entered. She came back with the Captain on her heels.

The Captain opened the half door and motioning Bobby in said, "Mr. Morrow, Con ta bai?" which is papiamento, the local language, for how are you, and raised his eyebrows slightly when Bobby responded, "Bon dia. Mi ta bon."

"I see that you are adjusting rather quickly to our little island, Mr. Morrow," the Captain said.

"Well I do enjoy it here and the people are fabulous."

· "What can I do for you today, Mr. Morrow?"

"Today, Captain Craane, it is what I can do for you. You are the head of law enforcement on this lovely island, and I am a mere guest. I have, however, discovered the source of drugs coming into your country and wanted to make you aware of him."

"Please, continue," the Captain said.

"There is an elaborate scheme using trained dolphins to bring the drugs onto your island. I do not know where they go after they come here, but I'm sure that you can easily find out, if necessary, or just close down their entry onto your island , whichever you see fit."

"Do you have any facts, Mr. Morrow."

"Yes, I do. Cordell Sherrod.." Bobby couldn't help but notice that the smile left the Captain's face, "is running the operation. The drugs come in from Venezuela via the dolphins to the old shrimp farm out near Lac Bay. I also think he may be the person that shot my friend Clint Armstrong, so I, and my government would certainly like to see him put away. Saying that, I appreciate that this is your country with your laws, and we would not presume to interfere with that. Whatever manner you choose to handle the situation will be fine with us."

The Captain studied a moment, "Mr. Morrow, you place me in a delicate situation."

"I don't understand, I thought you would be pleased that you can shut down a drug smuggling operation and make an example of the leader."

"In your country that would work nicely. Here in Bonaire where our entire island is only 24 miles long, 111 square miles and just 50 miles off the coast of Venezuela. Our defense consists of an occassional dutch cruiser which comes in and out of our port. We have no standing army just a few police officers. The Venezuelan drug cartels could invade our country with no problem, and you want me to take their leader into custody? Do I look like I have a death wish, Mr. Morrow?"

"I'm sorry, Captain, I thought you would be pleased that we gathered all the intel but then let you handle the situation."

"It's not that I am not pleased. more that I am helpless against that type of enemy."

The door to the Captain's office burst open, and the young Bonairean officer rushed to the Captain's side to whisper in his ear. He listened attentively then asked, "when?"

She whispered in his ear again, and he replied, "thank you. You may go."

"Mr. Morrow, I'm afraid you may be too late. Mr. Sherrod was just seen leaving the Armstrong lady's art gallery in a great hurry, with Mrs. Armstrong and your friend in tow. This is an unbelievable problem for us."

"Captain, if I may make a suggestion?" Bobby asked.

"Please, speak," the Captain said.

"If your getting involved with Sherrod is a problem, may I suggest that you allow me to handle the problem for you?"

"But we can no more let the American government come into our country and interfere than we can the Venezuelan government."

"I was not speaking of our government, Captain. Just me. And hopefully my dear friend, Richard. If we can capture Sherrod without your assistance and get him out of your country, neither the drug cartels nor the Venezuelan government can hold anything against you. You would quite simply not know anything about him or his drug smuggling operation."

"And if you fail, then I am left with American bodies on my island and a lot of interference from your government," the Captain said in an extremely disgusted tone.

"But, Captain. I'm sure I know where he is heading. I'm also sure there will only be him and his driver or whatever he is. At the moment I have the advantage of surprise on my side."

The Captain got up form his desk, clasped his hands behind his back and paced around his office. Bobby did not interrupt but did check his watch. After all the clock was ticking. If Sherrod had

Matty and Richard time would be of the essence. The Captain kept pacing. Then he stopped and looked straight into Bobby's eyes.

"Can your government assure me that you are not here. That there would be no retribution.?"

Bobby flicked open his phone and pushed the speed dial button.

"Colonel, Bobby, we have a situation." Bobby went on to explain all that he had just learned about Sherrod making off with Matty and Richard. Bobby listened and threw in the occassional, "yes, sir," then handed the phone to the Captain.

The Captain listened, then without saying a word hung up the phone and handed it back to Bobby.

"Sergeant," the Captain yelled.

The young lady in uniform ran into his office.

"Sergeant, please be so kind as to have an officer on patrol stop by Mrs. Armstrong's Gallery and close her door. She just called and apparently in her rush she may have left it open. Thank you, Sergeant."

As the door to the Captain's office closed, he looked at Bobby ,and said, "Mr. Morrow, it has indeed been a pleasure Not knowing you. Te aworo!"

Bobby replied, "Danki," and immediately left the office and the police station.

There were times between true professionals when a small glance or a mere facial expression can speak volumes and words are not necessary. There are also times when deniability is of utmost importance. Not saying something means it can be denied later on providing the perfect explanation if needed.

Bobby drove like a madman to the resort where he hurriedly parked the compact rental car and jumped into Clint's big old pickup truck with the boat in tow. Wasting no time he headed out E.E.G. Boulevard past the airport and turned onto Kaya IR Randolf Statuuis Van Eps, the shortcut over to Lac Bay. Mentally he took inventory of what weapons he had found in Clint's boat and truck and how he could approach the old shrimp farm without being seen. It was, after all, daylight, and in Bonaire that meant only one thing, plenty of sunshine and with the terrain consisting of lava, sand and a few cactus, there was certainly nothing to hide behind.

"It has been said that politics is the second oldest profession. I have learned that it bears a striking resemblance to the first.".............Ronald Reagan

Chapter 16

Sherrod's big black Lincoln flew past the entrance to the airport and made it's way down the island.

"I need to know," Matty said as she turned to face Sherrod, "did you shoot my husband?"

"You're better off without him," Sherrod answered.

"Did you shoot him?" she asked again, her voice getting louder.

"Yes, I shot him. I can't let my help have all the fun. And the old American saying is true - the bigger they are the harder they fall. He practically shook the island when the big tough guy fell over with his belly full of lead."

Matty went crazy. She managed to turn in the tight rear seat quarters and attacked Sherrod with both of her small fists hammering at his head and torso. Sherrod was unable to back away as he was jammed tight up against the door so he slammed his pistol into the side of Matty's head. Matty slumped over and

Richard grabbed her and pulled her close to himself. Sherrod aimed the gun at her head but Richard reached out and swatted it away.

"You want to shoot somebody, tough guy, you shoot me!" Richard said with no waiver in his voice.

"I may need you for now," Sherrod told Richard, "But it won't be long until you are expendable. Then, I will take great satisfaction in killing you. You Americans make me sick with your holier-than-thou attitude."

"Yes, well, I don't need a crystal ball to know that you don't have much of a future," Richard spat at the drug kingpin.

"Oh, is your famous Bobby Morrow going to ride in like a white knight and save your ass?"

"I doubt he'll ride in, but when you see him you better hope he is in the mood to cut you a break."

"Yes, well your tough guy Bobby Morrow is outnumbered," Sherrod said.

"That's funny, I only count you and your stupid driver up there."

"That's right. Our two guns against his one."

"Then he has you outnumbered asshole!" Richard spat at him. The back seat passengers all quickly leaned to the left as the Lincoln made a fast right turn onto the dusty, bumpy road leading up to the old shrimp farm. It skidded to a stop kicking up a cloud of dust. The huge driver jumped out and opened the door for his boss. Sherrod, keeping the gun trained on Richard spoke,

"get out slowly and take the broad with you. No funny stuff or you won't be alive when your friend Bobby comes."

"You better start soaking in this last little bit of Caribbean sunshine Sherrod cause you won't be enjoying it much longer," Richard told him as he slipped out the door of the Linclon being careful to hold on to Matty who was just starting to come around. As Richard pulled her out of the car she rubbed her head. Feeling the wetness on her fingers she looked at them, and saw the red blood. Her blood. Then she looked at Sherrod, "you bastard!"

"Get her in the building Mr. Richard St.Clair," Sherrod said as he motioned toward the door with his gun. The huge bodyguard was at the door holding it open.

Richard held onto Matty's arm as he guided her through the doorway. As Richard passed the driver, the huge man smacked Richard on the back of the head, then smiled. Richard stopped,glared at the huge man, then turned his head to look back to Matty. When he did he kicked him hard on the side of the knee. The driver fell like a sack of potatoes, grabbing his knee and howling in pain. Richard leaned down to give him some more when he heard the action of Sherrod's gun. Richard looked at Sherrod and smiled, "I was just going to help him up. He seems to have fallen'."

"I'll let you live long enough to help him inside. Any more tricks from you and the next bullet will have your name on it."

Richard yanked the oaf to his feet and helped him into the building. He was limping badly which made Richard sport a small smile.

"Okay St. Clair. Park him in that chair then get the duct tape off the shelf," Sherrod barked as he kept the gun pointed at Richard.

Richard deposited the driver then went to the shelf and picked up the duct tape. Then stood there, twirling the duct tape on his finger. "Want me to tape up the oaf's knee?" Richard asked sarcastically.

"No, but he is going to tape up your hands, so give him the tape then turn around."

Richard did as he was instructed. The driver slowly got to his feet putting all his weight on one leg and as roughly as possible taped Richards wrists together behind his back, then spun Richard around. The driver had a gleam in his eye but Richard stared him down.

"Touch me you tough guy and I'll wreck your other knee," Richard told him. The gleam left his eye.

"Tape up the girl," Sherrod told his driver. The driver hobbled over and taped her wrists together. Sherrod grabbed her by the arm again and turned her to face him. "Now be a good little girl cause you and I have some unfinished business," Sherrod told Matty. Matty spit in his face. Sherrod laughed as he wiped it on the sleeve of his expensive suit, laughing out loud the whole time.

Sherrod was about to say something when he heard the roar.

"Timid men prefer the calm of despotism to the tempestuous sea of liberty."........Thomas Jefferson.

Chapter 17

The Dodge Ram's huge V-8 motor was screaming as Bobby unleashed all the horsepower it had galloping down the narrow Bonaire blacktop pulling the trailer and Zodiac boat towards the boat ramp at Lac Bay. Several times he shot past locals slowly making their way along the highway and leaving them shaking their heads when the force of the wind from the truck and boat nearly blew them off the highway. Of course, being a small island where nearly everyone knew everyone else, they recognized the truck and boat as that of Wildman Armstrong's and had to be wondering for a moment whether or not he was still alive. Bobby turned off the highway onto the path leading to the boat ramp and swung a quick arc. Before even coming to a stop, he had the truck shifted into reverse and was backing the boat back towards the ocean as fast as possible. At the water's edge he slammed on the brakes, jumped out of the truck and raced to the boat trailer. He worked at breakneck speed unfastening the boat and shoving it off the trailer into the water. He checked the fuel in the big twin motors, grabbed the spare fuel can from off the boat and threw it into the bed of the pickup. Bobby pushed the Zodiac into the water, jumped on board and fired up the two huge Evinrude 300 motors and slammed the throttle forward standing the zodiac nearly straight up and flying out into the Caribbean Sea. After Bobby had pulled away from the shoreline he made a hard right turn and sped down the coast towards the old shrimp farm. It didn't take long at full throttle until he was upon the old shrimp farm. He manhandled the boat up against the concrete walls of the canal that fed into the old shrimp farm, cut the huge powerful motors off, threw the anchor and everything else he could find into the water and jumped up onto the narrow concrete wall. Bobby stood there in his usual confident manner and yelled, "Sherrod. It's Bobby Morrow. I'll give you one chance to live. You let my friends go unharmed and I'll let you go. I have a boat here that you can take to Venezuela."

"So the tough guy has arrived. Well, Mr. Bobby Morrow, I happen to be the person in charge. What say I shoot your friends then......" before Sherrod had a chance to finish his statement Bobby dove into the canal and was swimming underwater up it.

The driver looked to Sherrod. Sherrod motioned with his gun for the driver to go to the edge of the canal and check it out. The driver limped over and peered into the dark water. He pulled out his gun and shots rang out then he disappeared over the side of the canal. As the group watched a hand came up over the concrete wall followed by the top of a head of wet hair, followed by a gun aiming the laser sight directly at Sherrod. As the remainder of the head appeared Sherrod pulled Matty in front of himself so he could hide behind her and get the laser sight off his chest. But the steady laser sight merely honed in on his forehead as Bobby climbed over the side of the wall.

"Fat boy might need some help," Bobby said to Sherrod, "he's not much of a shot. I would have thought you could afford better help."

"Yes, well I am a good shot and I can't miss your friend Matty at this range," Sherrod said as he jammed the barrel of the gun into the side of Matty's head.

"So you shoot her, then I shoot you. What does that do for you? You're still dead!"

"Get back from the wall Morrow and go stand by your friend Mr. St.Clair," Sherrod said.

As Bobby moved over next to Richard, Sherrod moved to the canal keeping the gun on Matty and Matty between himself and Bobby.

"Sherrod, you will leave Matty here, or I will kill you," Bobby told him.

Sherrod just kept walking out to the end of the building where he could step around the wall onto the wall of the canal and flee to the boat. As he was about to step onto the canal wall he spoke to Bobby, "By the way, drop your gun."

"Can't do it. Sorry. Years of military training. The only way you get my gun is to pry it from my cold dead hand!"

"Then perhaps I'll shoot her now."

"Then perhaps I'll shoot you before your toes touch the boat," Bobby said then continued, "but if you let her go I give you my word I will not shoot you."

"I've heard that you are a man of your word. Let's find out," Sherrod said as he shoved Matty into the canal while he jumped onto the boat. He fired up the two huge engines and roared away from the shore heading straight for Venezuela.

"What the hell did you let him go for?" Richard asked Bobby.

"Just help help Matty out of the canal," Bobby answered as he cut the tape from Richard's wrist with his swiss army knife.

Richard jumped in the water and helped Matty out as she was struggling with her wrists still taped behind her back.

"Here, cut her loose," Bobby said to Richard as he tossed the knife his direction. Then Bobby ran over and dove into the canal. When he got to the end of the canal he disappeared underwater. Richard and Matty watched and waited for a few moments then Bobby burst through the water.

"What are you doing?" Richard yelled out to him.

"I'm going after Sherrod," he calmly answered.

"In case you haven't noticed he's in a very fast boat, that you gave him, I might add, and is heading to Venezuela. Now how do you intend to catch him?"

"I'm going to swim."

"You're going to swim?" Richard asked shaking his head.

"Yes. I left my diving gear here in the water," Bobby said as he drug the gear up onto the bank.

"And just how fast do you figure you can swim?" Richard asked sarcastically.

"Slow and steady wins the race, my friend."

"He is already out of sight," Richard reminded Bobby.

Bobby turned and looked out toward the Sea while he strapped on his tanks, "Yes he is."

"And you're going to catch him?"

"In about another two minutes, he's out of gas," Bobby said to Richard with a smile on his face.

Richard just shook his head then said, "but why did you let him go in the first place?"

"Captain Craane does not want him on his island and is not comfortable arresting him, so now he's off the island. And his driver can attest to that so keep him safe till I get back."

With that said, Bobby waded out into the beautiful blue Caribbean Sea and disappeared under the water.

Richard turned to Matty, "are you alright?"

"Yes, thank you," she said.

"Excuse me for a moment, I have to get the trash out of the canal."

Richard jumped into the canal and fished out the driver who had been clinging to the canal wall for dear life. Unable to use his one leg to push himself up, Richard had to push him up and over the wall. When Richard climbed out after him, he got the duct tape and duct taped the driver's wrists behind his back.

"There's another use for duct tape," Richard said to the soaking wet driver.

"When you can't make them see the light, make them feel the heat."......Ronald Reagan

Chapter 18

Diving in the warm Caribbean waters is exhilirating, but would be much more fun on the other side of the island. This was the wild side. The current was stronger, the marine life bigger and the water deeper. Bobby was headed for Blue Hole. He figured that with the small amount of fuel he left in the tank, and with those two big Evinrude 300's sucking it down, that Sherrod wouldn't get much further than that. So Bobby maintained a straight line and a nice consistent pace as he worked his way out to Blue Hole. He nearly collided with the huge Eagle Ray that swam toward him curious about who might be in it's hunting grounds. The Eagle Ray was about six feet across it's wingspan with the white dots covering it's gray smooth surface and the head which looks so out of place as it truly resembles the head of an eagle. Once it swam up to Bobby and saw he was not a threat, the Eagle Ray continued his hunt along the bottom for food. Several large barracuda followed Bobby but he knew they were just hoping he would scare out some food for them to catch. The bottom became deeper and the current stiffer but Bobby pressed on. He could see the wreck at Blue Hole in front of him and started looking toward the surface. After a few minutes he spotted the bottom of the rubber Zodiac boat floating on the surface. Figuring that Sherrod would be at the back near the engines, Bobby swam up to the front of the boat and slowly poked his head up out of the water. Bobby knew he had to be careful as Sherrod still had the gun and Bobby did not. All Bobby had was a knife strapped to his leg. Sherrod was slapping the motors, cursing in Spanish because they had sputtered to a stop and not knowing why or what to do. Bobby worked his way around the side of the boat so he could come up behind Sherrod. It would be too dangerous to try to slip over the side as his weight would shift the boat and Sherrod would know so he worked his way slowly back to where the motors and Sherrod was. While Sherrod was slapping the side of the engine, Bobby quickly reached out and grabbed his arm pulling him into the water. Sherrod dropped his gun in the excitement and went tumbling overboard into the deep blue Sea with Bobby pulling him downward. Sherrod kicked Bobby and swung his free hand but all the while Bobby was pulling him deeper. Sherrod managed to wriggle out of Bobby's grasp and swam like a shot to the surface and back onto the boat. He was still looking for his gun when Bobby came over the side of the boat.

"Thought you were a man of your word, that you wouldn't kill me," Sherrod said to Bobby.

"Correction, I said I wouldn't shoot you. And I won't, being a man of my word," Bobby said, "but I am going to feed you to the fish."

"Good luck with that Morrow," Sherrod spat.

Bobby casually pulled off his flippers and dropped the air tanks off his back. Before he had time to think Sherrod got into his martial arts stance and threw a kick at Bobby. Sherrod was a black belt and very adept at the martial arts as he spent most of his free time practicing on his employees. The kick knocked Bobby off balance and nearly off the back of the boat, but he fought to stay on his feet and inside the boat, while fighting to shake off the fierce blow that had just doubled him over.

"A coward is much more exposed to quarrels than a man of spirit."...... Thomas Jefferson

Chapter 19

The Colonel saw Bobby Morrow's number flash on the screen of his cell phone so he dropped what he was doing and answered it.

"Colonel, it's Bobby."

"What's up?" the Colonel asked.

"I'm on my way to collect Cordell Sherrod. He has taken Matty and Richard as hostage and I'm sure he is heading for the old shrimp farm. I'm in Clint's truck heading out there now."

"What's the plan?"

"Well," Bobby said as he sped along, "there is a fly in the ointment, Captain Craane does not want to be involved and wants

Sherrod off his island. So I thought we would do just that, get him off the island."

"What do you have in mind?"

"I can get him out to sea then stick him there for a few minutes, can you get me a team there to extricate him?"

The Colonel thought a second then replied, "I have a team in Curacao, I'll put them in a chopper now and send them over. Where is the meeting point?"

"I thought I would give him just enough fuel in the boat he is going to steal from me to get out to the Blue Hole area. I can't be too exact but that would be along a straight line to Venezuela, which will definitely be where he will run to when I let him escape."

"Blue Hole area, it is," the Colonel said, "what's the E.T.A.?"

"Allowing for me to get to the boat ramp, get the boat in the water, cruise down to the shrimp farm, confront Sherrod, let him motor out there; I would say about 60 minutes."

"The team will be there." The Colonel hung up. He had plans to make.

"Government does not solve problems, it subsidizes them."...........Ronald Reagan

Chapter 20

Bobby fought to stay in the bobbing boat in the Caribbean Sea with the waves pounding the boat and Sherrod pounding him with kick after kick. Ordinarily Sherrod would have put his victim down by now, Bobby was not an ordinary victim. Bobby Morrow, while normally a laid back, casual person, was a trained killer. He was far too stubborn to give in to having someone kick the crap out of him, and it was only a matter of time until he figured out the pattern. Which was just what happened. Sherrod changed legs each time he kicked. This time the right leg would be coming. This time, when it did, Bobby grabbed the toes of Sherrod's foot with his powerful right hand and the heel of Sherrod's foot with his equally powerful left hand. Bobby pulled downward with his right hand and upward with his left hand with all his might. The cracking noise floated out across the blue Caribbenan Sea. The pain shot up Sherrod's leg like lightning and came out his mouth in a terrifying scream as he crashed to the deck of the boat rolling onto his stomach to attempt to ease the pain. Bobby kept the pain coming then got in a kick of his own, pummeling Sherrod's mid section all the while still twisting the broken foot. Then Bobby threw the foot down to the deck causing another scream from Sherrod.

"Go ahead, finish me off," Sherrod managed between cries of pain.

"You're already finished Sherrod!"

"You'll have to kill me. Cause as soon as I can, I intend to kill you," Sherrod moaned, as he tried to crawl away from Bobby. Sherrod then grabbed the anchor and made a lunge at Bobby with it. Bobby sidestepped the swing but nearly lost his balance and went overboard. He was tempted to kill Sherrod then and there, after all, he was a drug pusher. He hooked little kids on his stuff and tore apart many a good family. The world would be better off without him. But Bobby wanted him punished slower, so he waited for the extrication team and let Sherrod lay on the deck whimpering.

It wasn't long before the helicopter showed up and a Navy Seal came flying down the rope and into the boat.

"Mr. Morrow, sir, the Colonel said you had some garbage you would like us to take off your hands," the Seal said to Bobby.

Bobby merely pointed to Sherrod. The Seal wasted no time tying Sherrod's hands with the plastic ties while another Seal joined them on the boat.

"That's not too tight is it?" the Seal asked Sherrod while he smiled. Sherrod just cried in pain.

"Where does it hurt?" the Seal asked.

Bobby responded, "he twisted his ankle."

Like a good doctor would do the Seal grabbed the misfigured ankle and gave it a little twist of his own, "is that where it hurts?" Sherrod screamed, both Seals smiled and Bobby just shook his head. The Seals then roughly strapped Sherrod into the harness and gave the sign to the chopper and Sherrod disappeared into the sky.

"Could you lower me down a little fuel?" Bobby asked the Seals.

"Yes, sir," the second seal responded and he immediately got on his waterproof phone and contacted the chopper. The rope immediately started down with a plastic can of fuel.

"You guys are better than AAA," Bobby said.

"Thank you, sir, and thank you for the gift," the Seal said as he smartly saluted Bobby.

"You don't need to salute me," Bobby said.

"Don't need to, sir, but want to, sir," The Seal replied as he assisted his teammate in getting in the harness which had come back down and quickly zipped the Seal back up. The rotors of the big sleek chopper had flattened the waves on the Sea around the boat and Bobby was struck by the calmness. The second Seal retrieved the harness as it made it's voyage back down again and efficiently got prepared then gave the chopper the thumbs up and he disappeared into the blue sky. The Seal wasn't even completely in the chopper when it dropped it's nose and took off like a shot. "Hi ho silver," Bobby said to himself and blushed with the pride that he felt for his fellow military men.

The calmness quickly disappeared, the waves began bouncing the boat around but Bobby maintained his footing and got the gas caps off the motors and the fuel can and with a little bit of splashing he managed to get the bulk of the fuel into the tank. He tossed the spare can aside. Fired up the two monster Evinrudes and at full throttle stood the Zodiac on it's tail and spun it around 180 degrees and headed for shore. He bounced off the tops of the waves and had but one thought in his mind. Getting to the airport and getting home to Ganister, Pennsylvania where he intended to squeeze his wife until she could hardly breathe. The Zodiac crossed the sea at a lightning pace and Bobby flew up onto the shore like marines invading a foreign country. He jumped out of the boat, pulled it clear of the surf, and jumped into Clint's pick up truck, turned the key, hit the throttle, and spun coral back into the Sea. In just a couple minutes he pulled into the old shrimp farm.

"Richard, you here?" he yelled as he entered the building.

"Where else would I be?" Richard shot back while Matty snickered.

"Where's the driver?" Bobby asked.

"In the car," Richard said. Bobby opened the car door but didn't see anyone. Richard walked to the back of the car and popped the trunk. The driver was taped and stuffed in the trunk. Bobby approached him and yanked him over so he could look into his face. Then Bobby pulled the diver's knife from his leg and went toward the driver. The big man attempted to squirm away but there was no room to move and though his mouth was taped you could hear him scream.

"Shut up," Bobby yelled at him, "act like a man."

Bobby then cut the tape off his wrists and ankles. The driver with his huge staring eyes kept close track of the knife in Bobby's hand and Bobby reached over and yanked the duct tape off the driver's mouth.

"Best to do it quick," Bobby said, "like taking off a band aid."

The driver just stared at Bobby, speechless, probably wondering when or how he would be killed.

"What are you doing with him?" Richard asked.

Bobby ignored Richard and said to the driver, "get out!"

The driver cautiously hauled his heft out of the trunk and the springs of the black Lincoln sighed as they popped upward. The driver stood there leaning on the trunk watching every move Bobby made.

"Where are the keys?" Bobby as no one in particular.

"Here," Richard said and he tossed them to Bobby who caught them without even looking in Richard's direction.

Bobby then handed the keys to the driver who reluctantly took them. He then looked at Bobby and said, "what now?"

"You're a driver, drive," Bobby said and he took a step back from the driver. The driver looked into each face then slowly moved towards the front of the car. As he opened the door on the driver's side of the car, he looked back at Bobby as if waiting for conformation.

"Get out of here. Your boss is already gone."

The driver wasted no time getting into the car, starting it up and he tore off out the lane toward the paved highway and freedom.

"Now what?" Richard asked Bobby.

"Matty has a gallery to run, you and I have a plane to catch. Let's go."

The trio left the building and squeezed into the cab of the truck while Richard said, "I'll drive! You're a terrible driver."

Bobby merely shrugged.

"Just stop at the airport," Bobby said, "then Matty can take her truck and come back for the boat. You don't mind do you Matty?"

"No, I don't mind. That you for everything you've done. It's nice to have some closure on Clint's death," she replied.

"You can get Russell to help you load the boat," Bobby told her.

"Of course, he's always willing to help," Matty said as she looked to Bobby, "but, one question."

"What's that?" Bobby asked.

"What of Sherrod?"

"He will be taking up residence in Guantanamo Bay? The Navy Seals are personally delivering him there."

"No chance he can escape?"

"Not from that crew. They would sure like him to try, but I'm sure he's smarter than that."

Matty sat back in the seat between the two friends and felt comfort for the first time in a long time.

Richard pulled the truck and empty trailer up to the front of the Flamingo Airport and jumped out. Followed by Bobby, then Matty.

"What about our luggage?" Richard asked.

"It will find it's way home. Trust me. The Colonel will see to it," Bobby replied as they took turns hugging Matty and stepped inside the open air terminal. Bobby walked over to the Delta desk and said to the young Bonairean girl in uniform, "Morrow and St.Clair, I assume you have tickets for us?"

She looked around her desk and found an envelope with their names on it which she handed to him.

"When does the flight leave?" Bobby asked.

"They have been sitting on the tarmac waiting for you," she said then asked, "who are you guys? Delta doesn't wait for anyone."

"Just two tourists from Pennsylvania," Bobby said smiling and turned to leave.

"Any luggage?" the girl asked.

"No. Thank you," Richard said as they each gave Matty one more hug and sauntered off to the waiting airplane. They walked through the customs area with no delays, were waved through by the immigration desk, and walked back out unto the warm Caribbean sunshine to cross the tarmac to the waiting airplane. The duo climbed the steps and stepped inside the plane and the air conditioning. The door was immediately closed behind them and the stewardess escorted them to their seats in first class.

As they were buckling their seat belts, Richard looked to Bobby and said, "damn, I'm going to fly with you more often. First class?"

"Nothing but the best for you buddy." Bobby replied.

"No free man shall be debarred the use of arms.".......Thomas
Jefferson

Chapter 21

The temperature difference was shocking when the plane landed at
Pittsburgh International airport.

"We should have brought coats," Richard said to Bobby as they
crossed the terminal, "I have to remember where I parked my car."

"The Colonel will have a car for us waiting," Bobby said.

"But what about my car?"

"We'll check with the driver," which is what they did when they saw the man holding the sign at the luggage carousel with their names on it.

"That's us," Bobby said to the sharply dressed man.

"This way gentleman," he responded and led the way out the doors into the frigid air but immediately opened the rear door of the limousine allowing them to get into the warm car.

"But what about my car?" Richard asked.

"I'm afraid your car is already in Ganister, Mr. St.Clair," the driver said.

"What do you mean by, 'I'm afraid'?" Richard inquired.

"Well the Colonel said that your Police Chief had it towed back to Ganister shortly after you left for the Caribbean."

"That, son-of-a..." Richard started to say but Bobby grabbed his arm.

"I told you not to toss the gun. Farr is determined to close that case and you and I are still both suspects. You especially because of the missing gun," Bobby told him.

"I just got back from the Caribbean and already you want to rain on my parade."

"We'll talk to him. We'll find out what he has and we'll get this thing settled. We both know who didn't shoot Billy Bollinger. We just have to figure out who did."

The two chatted as the driver knocked off the miles from Pittsburgh to Ganister and pulled into Bobby's driveway. Duke was waiting and shook all over with excitement as Bobby got out of the car, then rubbed up against him with his heft and nearly knocked Bobby over.

"Stay here tonight, Richard, and I'll take you home in the morning."

"I guess I could but I don't have any clean underwear."

"Claire will take care of it," Bobby said.

"Thanks for the ride," they both said to the driver, who got back into the car and started to drive off, then the back up lights went on and he backed up to Richard and Bobby.

"Oh, by the way, gentlemen," the driver said, "I'll be here to pick you up tomorrow afternoon at 3 sharp."

"For what?" Bobby asked.

"Because the Colonel told me to," the driver said as he rolled his window back up and drove off.

"What's that all about?" Richard asked Bobby.

"You got me. Guess we'll find out tomorrow."

Claire was waiting at the door in her housecoat and had already poured a cup of hot coffee for Bobby.

"Your tea is brewing," she said to Richard.

Bobby grabbed her around the waist and hugged her then gave her a long hard kiss.

"Don't mind me," Richard said to their backs, "maybe you two should get a room?"

"Fix your tea and be quiet," Bobby said when he came up for air.

When the couple pulled themselves apart, Claire said to Richard, "oh by the way, I had your blue suit picked up at your house today and brought over for tomorrow."

"What's tomorrow," Bobby asked her.

"All I know is the Colonel is having a small party at the Hite Winery north of Ebensburg and we are to be there," she replied.

"But, Richard, I have some bad news for you," she continued.

"What's that?"

"Your house is trashed."

"What?"

"When I went for your suit, I found it just trashed. Stuff everywhere, so I called the Colonel. He said that your Chief Farr had a warrant and was hunting your guns."

"That son-of-a...."

"That's the second time within a few hours that you have called him that. And you made him Chief! How ironic is that?" Bobby said.

"He's going to get ironic, up alongside his head."

"Well there's nothing you can do tonight so relax. Supper will be ready in a few minutes then you can get a shower and wash the salt off of you."

Claire prepared a nice dinner with roast beef, mashed potatoes, asparagus, and a fine Merlot to go with everything. The hot food, the quiet of the Morrow log home and the fire crackling in the fireplace brought sleep upon them all. Well, it did take a little longer for Claire and Bobby to get to sleep as they kissed goodnight and one thing led to another.

Duke wakened the household early the next morning as he defiantly stood in the middle of the driveway with his massive size barking at the police cruiser that was attempting to get to the Morrow residence.

"Duke," Bobby yelled at him, "get up here." Bobby waited on the porch in his jeans and coat but without any shoes on.

The police cruiser continued up the driveway and Chief Farr crawled out from behind the steering wheel.

"Morning, Chief," Bobby said, "come on in. It's cold out here." Bobby turned and went inside waiting for Chief Farr.

When the Chief came in and closed the door behind himself, he took off his hat and said, "I heard you two were home. I really need to talk to you both."

"Have a seat," Bobby told him, "you want a cup of coffee?"

Duke stood staring at the Chief. The Chief kept glancing over at Duke to be sure he was a sufficient distance away.

"He won't bother you," Bobby said, "well unless you've done something to piss him off. You didn't, did you?"

"I hope not," the Chief said, "but I did have to come with a search warrant and I don't think he likes me."

"You didn't give my wife any grief, did you?" The Chief looked away for a second. Just then Claire entered the kitchen.

"Morning Chief," she said to Farr.

"Morning Mrs. Morrow," the Chief said back, "I apologize if I upset you last time I was here."

"You didn't upset me, but I can't speak for Duke. He seems to be staring at you like you're a fresh hunk of meat."

"Anyway," Bobby said, "is there a reason you are here?"

Richard mozied into the kitchen and spied the Chief sitting at the table with his cup of coffee.

"You son-of-a...." he started to say but Bobby stopped him.

"Chief Farr," Bobby said, "it appears you have greatly pissed off your boss. Maybe something to do with towing his car from the airport. Or maybe with trashing his house. What do you think?"

"I had legal search warrants and thus far neither of you have been very forthcoming with me," the Chief replied.

"Yeah, well, when I get home, if my house is still trashed, you better be looking for a new job. And my Volvo better be in the same shape it was when I left it. If it isn't, after I fire you, I'll kick your ass!" Richard said very defiantly.

"Everything is fine, now," the Chief said, "the workers were there today after your Colonel got done raising hell with the whole town council. I may not have a job much longer anyway, because of that."

"Richard, sit down," Bobby said, "Chief, where are you in this investigation?"

The Chief responded, "first, I have questions for you two. You are my loose ends."

"We're not your loose ends, Chief," Bobby said, "'cause we didn't shoot Billy Bollinger."

"Then why is the Mayor hiding his guns?" the Chief asked as he looked to Richard.

"He's not hiding the gun. Gun, singular. One gun, but he is not hiding it, and he didn't shoot Billy," Bobby replied before Richard could speak.

"I have a witness. There were three cars that stopped at the scene where Billy's car was wrecked."

"Three?" Bobby asked.

"Yes, three. Richard's Volvo. Your old red truck and a silver car."

"Who's silver car?" Bobby asked as he perked up.

"I don't know," the Chief responded.

"Who is the witness?" Richard asked.

The Chief hesitated then said, "Grammy Guering."

"That makes sense," Bobby said, "she sits by that window and doesn't miss anything."

"She didn't recognize the silver car?" Richard asked the Chief.

"Any other witnesses?" Bobby asked the Chief.

"Not that I've found."

"Excuse me for a minute," Bobby said as he got up form the table and went into the open living room while he flipped his phone open and dialed a number.

"Yeah!" was the response on the other end of the line.

"It's Bobby."

"Yeah."

"Can I ask you a question?"

"Yeah."

"You doing any fishing?"

"Yeah."

"Down at the Juniata River?"

"Yeah."

"The day that Billy Bollinger was shot, were you fishing there?"

"Yeah."

"Can I come over and talk to you?"

"Yeah."

Bobby turned back to the the kitchen , "Chief, let's go."

"What do you mean, 'let's go?' I still have questions for you two."

"Chief, you're asking the wrong people questions, if you want to close this case, let's go," Bobby said, "come on Richard you're coming too."

"But we haven't had breakfast yet," Richard said to Bobby as he looked over to Claire with pleading eyes. Claire just shrugged as she continued drinking her coffee.

"Shit," Richard said and got up to go finish dressing.

As the trio was leaving the house, the chief asked, "where are we going Bobby?"

"Farmer Terry's," Bobby told him as the trio piled into the police cruiser. Richard glared at Bobby as he slid into the back seat.

"Why do I have to ride in the back?" Richard asked.

"Cause the Chief is driving," Bobby said, "And I'm not riding back there."

It was just a few minutes drive to Farmer Terry's, as he was popularly known. His real name was Terry Lee. He lived in an old farm house behind the Blue Hole, that massive deep blue puddle of water that at one time was a working gravel quarry. Fed by an underground stream the solid rock walled bowl contained forty feet of clear blue water. The narrow gravel road alongside the quarry led up to Terry's house. The road was in poor condition. Full of pot holes. Not because of inattention, but because it discouraged visitors, and Terry didn't like visitors. Terry liked to farm, hunt, fish, and be left alone with his family. The police cruiser bounced it's way up the lane and pulled up in front of the two story, hundred year old farmhouse.

As the Chief was getting out of the car, he was stopped by the sound of a shotgun being pumped.

Farmer Terry stood on the porch with the shotgun aimed at the Chief.

"What do you want?"

Then Bobby and Richard stepped out of the car.

Terry, seeing Bobby lowered the gun.

"Bobby. Richard," Terry said as he nodded his head toward them.

"Hey Terry," Bobby said, "How's it going?"

Terry looked at the Chief, "Not sure."

"I came to ask you that question, but wanted the Chief to hear you answer."

"Yeah. Ask."

"Were you fishing in the Juniata River when Billy Bollinger got shot?" Bobby asked.

"You already asked that question, Bobby," Terry answered.

"Tell the Chief," Bobby encouraged him.

"Yeah."

The Chief asked, "did you see anyone there?"

Terry ignored him. "What's your question, Bobby?"

"There was a silver car that pulled up before I pulled up. Did that person shoot Billy?"

"Yeah."

"Do you know who it was?"

"Yeah."

"Well why the hell didn't you report that?" the Chief asked in a raised voice.

The shotgun swung back up towards the Chief. "You weren't invited here! Just those two," Terry said.

The Chief shut up and looked to Bobby.

"Terry," Bobby asked, "who was driving the silver car?"

"That guy that runs the ambulance service."

"Shawn Boyer?" Bobby asked.

"Yeah."

"And he shot Billy?" Bobby asked again.

"Yeah. Stopped his car. Ran over to Billy's car. Pulled out a pistol and shot him. Then made a phone call and left."

"I ought to arrest you for withholding information," the Chief told Terry.

"And I ought to shoot you for trespassing," Terry responded.

The Chief looked at Bobby and jumped back into the car. Richard and Bobby thanked Terry for his hospitality. Before leaving Bobby asked, "Terry, your boy doing okay?"

"Yeah. He's a sniper now in the Army."

"I heard. I've been watching him move up through the ranks," Bobby replied.

"He wants to be just like you, Bobby."

"That's quite a compliment, but he needs to strive to be like his old man. You're a fine man, Terry."

"Stop by again," Terry said. "Don't bring him next time," he said as he motioned with the shotgun toward the Chief.

"He's alright," Bobby said to Terry as he got in the car.

"Let's go Chief," Bobby said as the Chief started the car and headed down the bumpy gravel lane.

"I still should arrest that farmer," the Chief said.

"Chief," Bobby said, "don't mess with Terry. You ever hear the old saying 'Never kick a sleeping dog?' You get in a pissing match with Terry and you'll be way out of your league. Trust me."

"I got a gun, too," the Chief remarked.

"Yes, but Terry won't hesitate to use his. Then he'll toss your body in the quarry."

The Chief decided to change the subject, "what possible motive could Shawm Boyer have to shoot Billy Bollinger?"

"Chief," Bobby said, "I've been investigating a drug ring in the ambulance service. That's why Billy Bollinger was getting out of town. I had evidence on him, I was just waiting for a bigger fish, and it makes sense that it would be his boss. So, take us back to my place then you go arrest Boyer and put this case to rest."

The Chief looked in the rearview mirror to Richard, "I'm sorry Mayor, I thought you shot Billy."

"I told you, I wanted to, but I didn't," Richard said, "you just make sure my car and house are back the way they belong.

"Do you think I'll get to keep my position, if I get this case closed?" the Chief asked Richard?

"You're not going to lose your position, Chief."

"But the way that Colonel raised hell with the council..." the Chief remarked.

"The Colonel will be sure that you don't lose your job, just go get that piece of scum in jail."

"To sit back hoping that someday, someway, someone will make things right is to go on feeding the crocodile, hoping he will eat you last - but eat you he will.".........Ronald Reagan

Chapter 22

The shiny black limousine pulled up the Morrow driveway while Duke watched from the porch where he was sunning himself. Duke raised his head at the sound of the gravel crunching under the tires, saw who it was, and went back to the chore of soaking up rays. The driver exited the vehicle and stood by the rear door until the Morrows and Richard came out of the house, then he opened the door for them. The trio was very dapper looking. Bobby in his blue suit with Claire in a matching dark blue dress and heels. Richard had on his black suit and colorful fish necktie.

"Watch the place while we're gone," Bobby said to Duke who lifted his head long enough to get his instructions.

The Lincoln cruised up the mountain to Ebensburg then got on Route 219 for a few miles before turning off the highway into the Hite Winery. The green grass was immaculately trimmed, the landscaping just perfect and the old former barn that was now the Winery was freshly painted. As the driver pulled up to the front entrance, a banner flapped in the light breeze, saying "Welcome, Senator".

Richard got out and assisted Claire as Bobby got out the other side.

"I guess the Senator is joining us," Richard said to Claire.

The trio entered and found a small group of people standing at the bar sampling wines. Upon hearing them enter the Colonel turned around and raised his glass towards them, "Welcome Senator St.Clair!" The group raised their glasses and toasted.

"What the hell are you talking about?" Richard asked the Colonel.

"We have placed your name on the ballot to run for Senator," the Colonel replied.

"But, why?"

"You have to be Senator for the next chapter of your life. For the greater good."

"But I thought I might start a bottled water company at the quarry, Blue Hole water."

"Who would ever buy bottled water?" the Colonel asked, "all you have to do is turn the faucet and water comes out?" the Colonel dismissed the idea with a flick of his wrist.

"Try the black raspberry-chocolate merlot or the pomegranate zinfandel, they are fabulous," Mrs. Hite told the group.

"Senator, huh?" Richard asked himself.

Thank you to those wonderful people who read my first two books: "The Blue Hole" which introduced Mayor Richard St.Clair and Bobby Morrow, the sometimes dentist, somtimes federal undercover agent.

"The Greater Good" where Bobby Morrow gets in the middle between terrorists and our own government.

Both books are available at www.amazon.com

A Special Thank You to my wife who has endured me pecking away on the laptop when she had other plans for me. And now, the white sands, blue water, and sunshine of Aruba are calling my name.

37077992R00076

Made in the USA
Middletown, DE
22 February 2019